Also by Sherrilyn Kenyon

(Listed in correct reading order)

The League

Generation 1

Born of Night
Born of Fire
Born of Shadows
Born of Silence

Watch for
Born of Fury
(coming 2014)

The League

Generation 2

Born of Ice
Fire & Ice

Dark-Hunter

Fantasy Lover
Night Pleasures
Night Embrace
Dance with the Devil
Kiss of the Night
Night Play
Seize the Night
Sins of the Night
Unleash the Night
Dark Side of the Moon

The Dream-Hunter
Devil May Cry
Upon the Midnight Clear
Dream Chaser
Acheron
One Silent Night
Dream Warrior
Bad Moon Rising
No Mercy
Retribution
The Guardian
Time Untime
Styxx

Chronicles of Nick

Infinity
Invincible
Infamous
Inferno

Watch for
Illusion
(coming 2014)

Lords of Avalon

(written as Kinley MacGregor)

Sword of Darkness
Knight of Darkness

SherrilynKenyon.com

For my husband for too many reasons to count.
For my boys who make me laugh and fill my life with joy.
For my friends who keep me sane.
And for my readers who mean so much to me.
Thank you all for being a part of my life and for filling my heart with love.

Author's Note

First, I want to be completely upfront and say that Cloak & Silence is about Ture and Maris, two men whose story captured my heart while I was writing *Born of Silence.* My books are always about the people who inhabit them and their struggles in life. Anyone who knows me will tell you that I respect all points of view. My father, and many members of my family, have shed their own blood and given their lives for our freedom to live our lives and to pursue our happiness as we see fit. And while I might not agree with the opinions of others, I would never spit on the sacrifice made by those who have given their lives for freedom by telling someone else they are not entitled to their beliefs.

I was very blessed that I was raised in a culturally mixed environment where I was able to grow up well versed in many different, often opposing opinions and lifestyles. It opened my eyes to many things. I didn't write this story to change anyone's opinion about anything. Again, I cannot stress enough that I believe we are all entitled to whatever viewpoint we hold.

I simply wrote this for Maris and Ture, and for those fans who wanted to know more about them and their relationship. If this is not your cup of tea, I respect that. I have many other books written about more traditional relationships and families. My own personal view is that life is hard for everyone. No one has an easy ride. But when you find that one person who will stand by your side while hell itself rains down on your head, that one person who won't betray your trust no matter what then life is much easier to suffer through. Those people are like unicorns—magical, and far too rare. But when you find your unicorn then you need to hold onto it. I grew up not believing in such mythological beasts. I thought them a lie told by others. Until the day when I found my own unicorn in the most unlikely of places—a late night college classroom. Over the years, my husband has more than proven to me that there are real people out there who have true integrity. People who will fight for others and who will stand strong against enemies and all the horrors life throws at you.

My one hope is if you don't already have such a special person in your life that you find one soon. Everyone, no matter who they are or where they come from, deserves to be loved and cherished for who and what they are.

IN MORTE VERITAS
LIVETHELEAGUE.COM

Chapter 1

"I'm telling you, Ture, he will come for us."

Ture scoffed bitterly at Zarya's blind optimism and devotion. "Honey, the only one coming for us is death, and I just hope the petty bastard stops on his way here and brings us a biscuit. . .Sooner rather than later."

Zarya rolled her eyes at Ture's acerbic tone and facetious humor. She wasn't sure at this point how long the two of them had been held. Since there were no windows in hell, she couldn't judge night from day, and while they slept between their torture sessions, she had no idea for how long. It never seemed to be more than mere snatches that were interrupted by severe pain and utter misery.

Her entire body aching, she winced at the sorry condition Ture was in. He'd always been so fastidious with his appearance. Never so much as a strand of dark reddish brown hair out of place.

But today that hair was matted with blood and gnarled with tangles. His gorgeous face was bruised with one eye swollen completely shut. Someone had left a perfect image of a handprint in the form of a bruise along his chiseled jawline. Worse were the handprints where he'd been choked.

Repeatedly.

Guilt racked her. But for her and her stupidity, he wouldn't even be here. *It's all my fault.*

Under no circumstance should she have asked him to don a Resistance uniform. For that one favor to her, the League had assumed him to be one of her men and no matter how much she tried to tell them the truth, no one listened. They continued to torture him for information he didn't have, and her for information she refused to give.

"I'm so sorry I got you into this."

Ture wanted to curse Zarya for her naive stupidity in thinking she could pull off a peace mission between lunatics. He really did. But as he looked at her and saw the sincerity in her gaze—her agonized guilt over the pain she'd caused him—his anger vaporized. In all the universe, she was the closest thing to family he'd known in a very long time. And that was how he'd gotten caught up in this mess.

For her, he would do anything.

Sighing at his own epic stupidity, he opened his arms to her and she quickly accepted the invitation for a hug.

In spite of the pain caused from her body touching his, he held her to his chest. She tucked her head beneath his chin like his sister had done when she was a little girl just returning from her treatments. How he hated his own weakness. Mara had been everything to him and he still mourned her. Zarya reminded him so much of her that he, who had sworn to let no one back into his life, had been an utter fool for her from day one. He was that way with any woman in pain.

A sucker to the extreme.

And the last thing he wanted to do was lose another family member he loved.

"You have to tell them what they want to know, Z."

"I can't. They want me to give them the names of the Sentella High Command."

The Sentella was the only organization in existence that

truly threatened the League's iron grip on their United Systems. They alone could break the League apart and free the governments that lived in fear of the League's tyranny. But this wasn't about the freedom of people who wouldn't spit on them if they were on fire.

This was about their own survival. The League interrogators had already killed her once. Next time, they might not revive her.

He brushed the bloody hair back from her face. "You need to think of your baby, honey. You're lucky you haven't miscarried already."

Still, she held on to a blind hope he couldn't even begin to fathom. "Darling will come for us. I know he will."

Ture ground his teeth at her childish devotion. Not once since they'd been taken had it faltered. She honestly thought her boyfriend would come risk his own life and free them from this hellhole.

How he wished he could believe it, too. But he knew better. "Heroes aren't real. They don't come charging in to save their damsel. Trust me. They vapor trail off at the first sign of trouble, leaving you behind to face the invading army all by yourself, hoping they'll burn the house down on top of you so they don't have to deal with you again."

"No, Ture. Those are selfish assholes. A hero doesn't give up or give in. Ever. Darling told me he would crawl naked through Kere's fiery and frigid domain, over broken glass, just to hold my hand, and I believe him."

"Men will say anything to get into your pants, love. They don't mean a word of it."

She took his hand into hers and held it tight. "I'm sorry that you've never been in love with a man who really loved you back, Ture. But I'm telling you. . .I have seen what Darling and Maris have gone through for each other, and they won't leave us here. They won't rest until they've rescued us. I know it."

Ture opened his mouth then closed it. There was no need in arguing. She had her delusions and he had his.

Maybe there had been a time in his life when he'd been so blinded by love that he, too, believed such bullshit. But too many years of being bitch-slapped by selfish dicks had taken its toll on him.

Not even his own family had ever been there when he needed them. So why should a stranger?

People, by their very natures, were users. That was just the way it was.

But in spite of his past, he wouldn't take away the only thing that gave her comfort in this unending misery. Let her have her delusions while she could. He tightened his grip, his heart breaking for her, and for the letdown she'd set herself up for.

They had actually killed her today during her torture and then brought her back just so they could continue on with it.

Damn them all for their cruelty.

"I hope you're right, sweetie," he breathed against her hair. The last thing he wanted was for her to learn the harsh lessons that had been rammed down his throat with a violent fist. He wept for the loss of anyone's innocence, especially when the loss was brutal. And deep down in a place he hated, was that last vestige of his own hope that she was right. That maybe, just maybe, there were people in the world worth something. Someone who could stand by you even in hell and not betray you.

Yeah. . .

"Zarya?"

"Mmm?"

He cleared the knot in his throat as he asked a question that made him hate himself and his own blind optimism even more. "Tell me what it's like to be held by someone who really loves you."

Zarya swallowed hard. His request wrung her heart. While almost everyone she'd ever loved had been brutally murdered, Ture's family had abandoned or disowned him. Or worse, they used him. Because of that, he'd had an even harder time trusting people than she did. No matter what, he expected the people around him to turn on him.

The saddest part?

They always had.

"It's the most wonderful thing you can imagine. There's truly nothing like it."

He sighed wearily. "I don't know how you can take such a beating and still protect him."

How could she not? Darling would do the same for her, and then some. She had no doubt. He really was *that* kind of man. "Did I ever tell you what my mother's last words were to me?"

He shook his head.

"It was the morning when she went to confront my father's killer. I asked her why she wouldn't let one of the soldiers or gerents handle his rescue. And she said to me that all little girls, regardless of what they say, dream of a prince to come in and sweep them off their feet and save the day. But what no one ever mentions is that all little boys dream of a princess to do the same thing for them. But the problem with princes and princesses is that they're spoiled and self-absorbed. They act in their own best interest. They don't go after their loved ones to rescue them so much as they do it for their own vainglory, and to serve themselves. While she'd had many princes try for her hand, it was a king who had claimed her heart. Unlike princes, kings take responsibility. They think of others instead of themselves and they will risk everything, even their very lives, for those they love. It is never about them, but rather about the ones they cherish most. They love to such depth that they would sacrifice all just to see their family smile. For every thousand princes, there is only one king. And such rare men do not deserve a useless princess who sits on her duff and orders others to worship her and do her bidding. Kings deserve queens—rare women who never flinch to do whatever it takes to keep their king safe. Women who have the courage to face any attacker and to rally to whatever challenge life throws at them. I will not sit here, she said to me, and let your father suffer while I hide in comfort. He risked his life to keep us safe and I will do no less for him. If it means my life, so be it. After all, he is my life and I don't want to live without him. He deserves only my best and that's exactly what he's going to get, no matter the personal cost."

Ture drew a ragged breath as the tears welling in her eyes choked him. "Though I never had the pleasure of meeting her, I love your mother. You know that, right?"

She squeezed his hand as her tears began to fall. "I love her, too. And I've tried every day of my life to do her proud and to be the queen she wanted me to be."

He kissed the side of her head. "Sweetie, you are better than any queen. You're a freedom fighter for our people, and if your Darling is the king you think him to be, you will live to be an empress."

"Then I shall be an empress. You will see."

Ture smiled at the sincerity of her tone. How she could still believe in fairytales after everything life had tossed in her face, he had no idea. "Fine then. Just make sure when you're empress, you find a king for me."

"I will."

Ture tightened his grip on her as she went limp in his arms. Fear seized him until he assured himself that she was still breathing.

Thank the gods she wasn't dead. That was something he couldn't even bear to contemplate. Never in his life had he known anyone as precious and loyal as Zarya.

But she wouldn't be able to survive much more. For that matter, neither would he. Every day got harder. They couldn't break him because he knew nothing. They couldn't break her because she was the most stubborn creature alive.

He admired that even though it made him want to wring her neck.

His one greatest hope was that her Darling was the

king she'd convinced herself that he was. In Ture's world, such men didn't exist. They were fables and lies.

Still, he couldn't stop imagining a world where people didn't disappoint each other. A world where you could put your life and heart into the hands of another and not fear betrayal or harm. A universe populated by people like Zarya. . .

You sound like an old woman.

He felt like an old man. Jaded. Cold. Aching. He licked at the blood on his lips and forced his thoughts away from things he knew were lies. Things that were impossible. People sucked. They were users and no matter how much you gave, they never stayed.

Closing his eyes, he prayed for death. And why shouldn't he? He had no reason to live. Nothing to live for. Life was just something you suffered through to reach the other side.

And he was so tired now. . .

On the edge of his falling asleep, a loud and rude noise blared outside their cell. At first, he thought it was another form of torture.

Until he realized it came from the yard and there were soldiers responding.

He scowled at the strange sounds.

An attack?

No. It couldn't be. No one attacked a prison. Ever. It must be another escaped prisoner who would be gunned down soon.

Yet there was no denying the blaring warning siren or the sound of running feet and shouts that they were under attack. Hoping he was right, he shook Zarya awake.

"Do you hear that?" he asked her.

Zarya could barely understand Ture's words. Something kept buzzing in her head and it wouldn't stop. "Hear what?"

A blast hit their door. At first she thought she imagined it.

Until it struck again.

And again.

Could it be. . .?

No. You're dreaming. It's not real. Just a hallucination brought on by your fever and pain.

In her mind, she saw Darling carrying her out of this nightmare like he'd done when she'd sprained her ankle in the palace kitchen. Of him holding her close and telling her it was over and that she was finally safe.

I swear, if I ever get out of this I will never leave the palace again.

A heartbeat later, the door in front of them lifted. Smoke billowed into the room, filling it instantly. She choked and coughed, trying to breathe around the odor.

Ture held her close as two League soldiers spilled into the room then turned to speak to another soldier who stayed in the hallway, firing at targets Ture couldn't see. He was ready to fight them to the bitter end if they tried to take either of them again, but they didn't move closer.

Preoccupied with whatever was happening in the hallway, neither of soldier even looked at them.

"Grab the woman!" Someone shouted from outside their cell. "We have to have her or we can't leave."

The two soldiers came toward them then.

Zarya's heart pounded as she tried to understand what was happening. Aching to the point it hurt to breathe, she didn't move until they closed in on her. In their hurry earlier to dump her and run, they'd forgotten to handcuff her.

Their mistake.

She reverted to her strict military training. Grabbing the blaster from the first one to reach her, she used it to shoot his partner.

Shrieking, the soldier hit the deck and died.

Before she could move, the one she'd grabbed brought his fist down across her face with a blow so fierce, it made her head explode with pain. The room spun, nauseating her.

Ture lunged at him and slammed him back against the wall as more soldiers poured into the room.

Zarya fought as hard as she could, but she was injured and outnumbered. Still, she didn't let it daunt her. Her father had taught her to fight no matter how bad she ached.

There were more battle sounds out in the hallway.

Ture moved to cover her. Though he lacked her skill, he was by no means weak. Nor helpless.

A new group of soldiers rushed them. Zarya leveled her blaster at them and pulled the trigger, only to discover it was out of charges.

Ture cursed under his breath. Leave it to his luck. . .

Turning the blaster around in her hand, she intended to use it as a blunt object. But the men didn't make it to them. Before they could reach her or him, blasts struck the soldiers and sent them to the ground at their feet.

Ture put himself between Zarya and whatever new threat was coming for them.

A second later, the smoke cleared to show another fighter in a burgundy battlesuit checking the fallen League soldiers for life signs.

This new soldier had barely stepped inside before he was attacked by three more League soldiers.

Even though he was wounded in multiple places, the newcomer used skills that defied description. He turned and caught the first League soldier with a blow so hard, he shattered his attacker's nose. The next one, he flipped and stabbed. The third soldier paused as he saw what awaited him in the bodies that were littered all over the room.

Eyes wide, he ran outside.

The newcomer turned to face them.

Ture wasn't sure what to make of him as he looked to Zarya to see if she knew this one. One glance and it was obvious she'd never seen him before.

Damn.

Bleeding profusely from several wounds, the newcomer froze the instant he saw them. Then he spoke in a language Ture didn't recognize.

More blasts ricocheted in the hallway behind him.

In one smooth, impressive move, the soldier hit the floor, slid on his knees and spun around to shoot the three guards who ran in behind him. Without hesitating, he body rolled until he came to a stop by their side.

Ignoring Ture, he touched Zarya's shoulder with a gentle hand. "Zarya?"

Tears filled her eyes as she sobbed and fell into the soldier's arms. "Maris?"

Maris. . .

Ture's heart pounded at the name of the man she'd talked about for countless hours. In her esteem, Maris was second only to her beloved Darling.

The newcomer holstered his weapon. "Can you walk, honey?"

Before she could respond, the room was invaded by even more League soldiers.

Jerking his weapon out again, Maris jumped to his feet and opened fire, forcing the soldiers back into the hallway. Oblivious to the fact that he was wounded, he fought on. Ture had never seen anything like it. How could Maris stand so strong and bleed like that?

But even more incredulous was the fact that Maris had come to rescue them. Period.

Zarya had been right. There were decent humans in the universe after all. Who'd have ever guessed?

As soon as Maris set the League soldiers fleeing, he returned to their side.

Ture helped Zarya to her feet. She took one step before her legs buckled. Faster than Ture could blink, Maris scooped her up into his arms. "Don't worry, sweetie. I've got you."

Ture hissed as he saw the targeting laser appear on Maris's uniform. Without thought, he jumped in front of it. But no one fired.

Instead, a man dressed in a black Sentella uniform stood in the doorway as if frozen in place.

"Zarya?" he breathed. His tone that of a prayer.

Maris nodded.

"Darling?" Zarya said, her voice breaking as she reached for him.

Ture couldn't move as he stared in total disbelief. God love her, she'd been right to put her faith in her king. In spite of his family name and birthright, Darling Cruel was everything she'd said and then some.

Stunned to the deepest level, he watched as Maris handed her off to Darling who held her as if she was the most precious thing in the entire universe.

Gods, to have one person hold him like that. . .

"I knew you'd come for me," she sobbed, laying her hand against Darling's helmet that kept his identity completely hidden from his enemies. "I knew it."

Ture caught himself against the wall as the room spun. For a moment, he thought he'd go down. But by some other miracle, he stayed on his feet. "She never once lost faith in you, Majesty."

All of a sudden, Maris was next to him, helping him to catch his balance. He pulled Ture's arm around his shoulders and held him close.

Still, Ture couldn't believe they were here. "I told her it wasn't feasible. That you'd never find us, but she was right. She said you'd promised her that you would bust hell itself open to get to her. And that you never lied." Ture tried to take a step, but it was useless. His battered body was through.

Ture fully expected to hit the floor.

He didn't. Instead, Maris swept him up in his arms and held him.

Maris tightened his grip to keep him safe. "Don't worry. We'll get you to help."

It was inconceivable. Ture frowned at the blood on his hand that hadn't come from him or Zarya. "You need a medic as much as I do."

Even though he had him fully cradled, Maris shrugged. "It's not as bad as it looks."

Yeah, right. At six foot one, Ture was anything but small. And while he was lean, he was all muscle and not light of weight.

Yet Maris carried him past Darling and Zarya as if he weighed nothing at all.

Just as they reached the door, a shot went past them.

Zarya had used Darling's blaster to drive back another League soldier.

Maris fell back into the room, spun with Ture in his arms and then set Ture down on the floor. "They're coming fast and furious," he warned the others.

With an obvious reluctance, Darling placed Zarya on the ground beside Ture. "Let them bring it with all they have. You ready, Mari?"

Maris answered with laughter in his tone. "You know I hate fighting. But I think a little payback for my damaged battlesuit might actually make me feel better for once."

"I know it'll do great things for me." Darling pulled a fully charged blaster off his holster and exchanged it for the one Zarya had shot. "Stay behind us."

Maris handed one of his blasters to Ture. "Do you know how to shoot?"

Ture scowled at the foreign feel of the weapon in his hand. Ironically, his father had tried to teach him for years and he'd always sucked terribly. He offered a lopsided grin at Maris. "Not straight. . .in more ways than one. But if I aim at their feet I can hopefully wound them until one of you finishes them off. And that way if I really miss, I won't kill an ally. You'll just limp a little."

Maris laughed. "Thanks for the consideration. I'm Maris Sulle, by the way, and I should probably warn you that it didn't go well for the last guy who accidentally wounded me."

With Maris's air of bad ass machismo, Ture could just imagine. And he was doubly glad he wasn't the one who'd shot him. "I'm Zarya's friend, Ture Xans."

"Nice meeting you."

Well at least Maris had manners. Even in the middle of battle.

Darling tapped his link. "Hauk? Are you still evacing the civs?"

"Yeah. Are you pinned?"

"No. We're coming out of the last cell. I just didn't want you to shoot us by mistake. I know how caught up you get in a fight."

Hauk hissed. "Why are you bitching about that again? I only shot you once and it was an accident caused by your premature explosion problem. Had you not startled me while I was changing our charges, it wouldn't have happened."

"Anyway," Darling said, ignoring the outburst. "There are four of us. Don't fire."

Darling turned back to them. "Can you two walk at all?"

"Are you kidding?" Zarya asked. "Right now I could fly."

Nodding, Ture agreed. "To get out of hell, I'd skip to the beat of the worst song ever recorded. Even if it means dragging my entrails behind me."

Darling snorted. "We'll go slow and if your entrails happen to start dragging, please let us know." Then, he and Maris headed for the door.

"Stay put and we'll be right back for you," Maris said.

For the first time ever, Ture believed those words.

Ture waited behind with Zarya while Darling and Maris opened fire and made a pathway for them. Fearless and skilled, they moved in total synchrony.

Impressed with both their skills, Ture frowned at Zarya. "Are you sure Maris is gay?"

She smiled at him. "Absolutely."

Ture wasn't so sure. Not that he believed in stereotypes of any kind. He'd known many gay men who didn't betray themselves. At least not to outsiders. But with Maris. . .

He really hid it well.

Maris returned to help them to their feet while Darling stood guard at the door.

They stayed behind Maris and Darling with Zarya giving cover fire while they walked slowly down the hall then up the stairs with Darling and Maris taking turns to help them. Ture's head was light and his stomach churned. Worse, the stench of burning wires aggravated his nausea.

Please don't let me be sick. Not when they were so close to finally getting out of here. He wanted nothing to delay this escape. Especially not with something that would make him look weak in front of Maris and Darling.

No sooner had they reached the upstairs landing than the entire building went dark. Maris and Darling fell back to cover them.

Darling swapped out his charges. "We're on our way," he said to someone who must have spoken to him through his link. "Just a few minutes more."

They moved forward again.

As they rounded a corner, a group of assassins opened fire. Darling shielded Zarya while Maris covered Ture.

"Don't worry," Maris said softly to Ture as he placed a hand on his uninjured shoulder. "I'm not going to let anything happen to you."

Those words stunned him as much as Maris's possessive hold. He wasn't used to people who didn't toss others out to protect their own asses.

Darling cursed. "I could really use the tricom right now."

Zarya offered him an apologetic grimace. "Sorry. It was broken when I was taken."

"Figures." Darling cleared the assassins with a small bomb then nodded to Maris. They started moving again.

Slowly, they made their way down the hall until they met up with Nemesis who was helping a large group of prisoners get to safety.

Ture froze as he caught sight of the most feared free assassin known. This was a creature who had mercy on no one. It was said he'd even murdered his own father. Just for practice. And while Ture was far from small, this creature towered over him.

Holy shit. . .

Even so, Darling and Maris greeted him like a friend.

"Is everyone out?" Darling asked the legendary killer.

Nemesis nodded. "The last group is coming down behind you, right now."

Thank the gods Nemesis was on their side. But still. . .

This day couldn't get any more surreal or bizarre.

Prisoners and Sentella soldiers filled the hallway. To his utter shock, Maris cupped Ture's cheek in his gloved hand. "You still with us?"

Ture nodded as his vision dimmed. How he wished he knew what Maris looked like. But right then, Maris could have two heads and reptilian skin and he'd be beautiful to him.

Maris checked Ture's pulse. "Catch your breath, sweetie. We're almost out of here. Just lean on me as much as you need to."

How pathetic that those words were the kindest thing anyone had ever said to him.

More than that, Maris draped Ture's arm around his shoulders and held him tight against his side while he kept his other hand free to shoot.

Suddenly, the walls around them flickered and blinked as someone turned on the video monitors. Out of nowhere, a man's face appeared all around them, on every wall. Floor to ceiling. Handsome and cruel, the man had one eye covered by a patch.

Maris cursed under his breath.

"Who is it?" Ture asked him.

"Kyr Zemin. High Commander of the League and my idiot brother."

Now there was something Zarya had neglected to tell him. The man she'd been scheming to set him up with was related to the very nutcase who'd held and tortured them.

That didn't bode well for Maris's mental stability. Which meant Ture would fall in love with him and then get his ass kicked for it.

A furious tic beat in Kyr's jaw. "Do you know who I am?"

Nemesis snorted derisively. "We know. We just don't give a shit."

Curling his lip, Kyr raked him with a repugnant glare. "You have breached the sanctity of one of our prisons. Have you any idea the sentence you've brought down on your heads?"

Now it was Darling's turn to scoff. "Add it to the other twelve dozen death sentences we carry."

Kyr's tic picked up speed. "I don't think you truly understand the magnitude of what you're doing. Return my prisoners to their cells or—"

"Fuck. You," Darling snarled, punctuating each word.

Kyr's nostrils flared. "Those prisoners do not belong to you. They are League property. You have absolutely no right to them."

Before anyone realized what he was doing, Darling snatched his helmet off and threw it to the ground so hard, it bounced three feet high.

Maris's grip on Ture tightened. "Damn his temper. How can you love someone so much and still want to put your foot up their sphincter?"

Ture had no idea, and Kyr held the same shocked expression he was pretty sure marked his own face. While everyone around them, including Kyr, was rendered speechless and spellbound by Kere's real identity, Ture's shock came from the stupidity of Darling revealing himself to the one person who could seriously screw up his life.

But what made Ture want to choke Darling most was the fact that Zarya had been tortured for a secret he'd just callously revealed. She should have saved herself the misery and given it up the first day they were taken.

Fearlessly stupid, Darling went straight to the wall on the right and leveled a killing glare at Kyr. "The hell you say. They are *my* people, not yours. You sent your army into my territory and took not just my citizens, but *my consort*. How dare you!"

Kyr gave Zarya a look that said she hadn't bathed in a month or more. "She's not your consort."

Darling shook his head in denial. "She wears my ring and was officially bound to me when we were children—something sanctified and approved by your predecessor."

Zarya gasped at his unexpected disclosure.

Ture gaped. Was any of that true?

"By all laws," Darling continued, "she is my consort. And five minutes after I get her home, she will officially be my wife."

Kyr arched a daring brow. "So you're declaring war on us, then."

Yeah, there was no going back now.

But Darling was nothing, if not a brilliant politician. "Interesting concept. I would say that you declared it on us when you marched your army into *Our* empire and destroyed *Our* property, and kidnapped *Our* citizens. And now *We're* answering it. No one seizes my people. I don't care who you are."

"The League was invited in by your own council who wanted *you* removed from power."

"Were you?" Darling asked with a hint of laughter in his voice. "That's not what I heard. In fact, I have the entire CDS who will swear they never asked for you to intervene. That you took it upon yourself to attack us."

Kyr slammed his hand down on his desk. "You have no idea what you're unleashing right now, *verikon.*"

Ture had no idea what that word meant, or the language it belonged to, but from Darling's reaction, it was obvious he knew it well.

And it wasn't a compliment.

"And neither do you, *ciratile.* You ever try this shit again with me and mine, and I will rape and plunder the village, and burn the motherfucker to the ground. . ." He looked around at the bodies on the floor. "And as you've seen here today, there ain't nothing you bitches can do to stop me. Talk is cheap. Pain is free. And I'm peddling the shit out of it. So you come on and get some."

Kyr laughed as if he relished the thought. "War it is. Good luck, *Your Majesty*," he sneered that title. "No one will ever support you in this. You're about to find out what happens to nations that fight alone."

Nemesis jerked his helmet off and moved to stand beside Darling. Ture's jaw went slack. Nemesis was the Andarion prince and heir, Nykyrian Quiakides?

Get the hell out of town. Who would have ever guessed *that*?

Stunned even more, he held his breath as Nykyrian shook his head. "You would be wrong there, Zemen. Not only does he have the full backing of Nemesis and the Sentella, he has that of my people. From both sides. Human *and* Andarion."

"And you can add mine to it, too," another Sentella member said as he exposed his face. Again, Ture gaped at the sight of the Exterian prince, Caillen. "The Exterians fear nothing, and I'm pretty sure the Qillaqs will back us, too. After all, they love a good fight. The bigger, the bloodier, the better."

None of the others exposed their faces, but they stood shoulder to shoulder behind Darling. "The Tavali will always fight for and back the Sentella, especially against the League."

Oh yeah, this was going to be one bloody war these people were starting.

And all for a woman he'd called a fool for her belief that someone could love her enough to rescue her, never mind start a war over her capture.

Wow. . .

Kyr took a full minute before he spoke again. "All of you will regret this."

Darling smirked. "The war is on. Can't wait for our first dance."

An instant later, the screens went dark.

"How rude!" a female soldier tsked. "It's a good thing he's on the other side of the Nine Systems, otherwise, I'd have to hunt him down and hurt him."

The man who stood beside Nykyrian let out an evil laugh. "Yes, but not rude on his part." He held up his wrist computer. "I killed the feed. Five more seconds of looking at him and I'd have puked." He turned his attention to Darling. "Remind me later that we really need to send you to anger management therapy."

Darling widened his eyes innocently at the man as he pulled Zarya against him. "I have no idea what you're talking about, Rit. I'm all good."

"Yeah, but we're not," another insanely tall man said. "We just got busted."

One of the Tavali soldiers draped an arm around his shoulders. "We're not busted, brother. Only the morons who showed their faces." He passed a pointed stare to Nykyrian, Darling and Caillen.

Caillen shrugged. "What the hell? I never liked feeling safe, anyway. That's for old women."

The female who'd spoken came down the stairs, holding another man against her. Darling rushed toward them. "What happened?"

"He protected me and got shot."

"I'll be fine," the man said with a grimace.

"Thought you weren't psychic?" Darling asked.

"I'm not. But I know my body and right now, my head really hates you, Dar." He winced in pain as he met Zarya's gaze. "Don't worry. You're both fine."

Bursting into tears, she rushed to hug him. "Thank you! I've been so scared."

Ture frowned at her reaction.

The man patted her on the back then stepped away. "Darling? You really should show her those papers you found."

Darling sighed. "I hate it when you do that, Nero."

"I know. Now I need to lie down."

Ture felt the same way.

The tallest soldier among them went to take the man from the woman's grasp. "Let's all get out of here before reinforcements come. Kyr may be on the other side of the universe, but not all of his army is with him."

Maris nodded before he picked Ture up and carried him out of the prison and into their waiting transport.

Just outside the door, Maris turned toward another soldier who was walking past. "Hey, Drake? Can you tow my ship out of here for me?"

Drake, who was completely covered by his battlesuit, launched himself up the ramp to stand beside them. "Are you hurt too badly to fly?" There was no missing the concern in his tone as he scanned Maris's body and touched several of the injuries to inspect them. For some reason, Ture felt a vicious stab of jealousy. Drake must be Maris's boyfriend.

"I'm fine, baby. I just have someone more important to take care of."

"Okay." Drake patted Maris on the shoulder. "Let me know if you need anything else."

Ture stared at the hand that lingered on Maris's body. And he wondered if Drake knew how lucky he was to have someone like Maris in his life.

All Ture had ever found were selfish dickheads who never hesitated to verbally stab him.

As Drake left, Maris carried Ture into the ship, to a small room where he could lay him down on a small bed in the infirmary. He moved to get a blanket.

"I hope I didn't get you in trouble with your boyfriend."

Maris froze as he tucked the blanket around his body. "Huh?"

"Drake. . .outside. I hope he's not the jealous type."

He burst out laughing. "Trust me, Drake is *not* my boyfriend. I'd have to murder myself if he were. He's more like a kid brother I've known for most of his irritating life." Stepping back from the bed, Maris hit the release for his helmet then pulled it off.

For a full minute, Ture couldn't breathe as the full impact of Maris's looks overwhelmed him. His face finely boned and well chiseled, Maris was male beauty personified. Deep, dark eyes held him captive as they betrayed the depth of Maris's intelligence and zest for life. The sweat from battle had left his short dark hair plastered to his head, but it didn't detract from his handsomeness at all. Rather, it made him even more appealing, more masculine. Yet it was those plump full lips that made Ture's throat go dry. Lips he wanted to taste so badly that for a moment, it drove away all thoughts of pain.

Damn. . .

He should have let Zarya introduce him to Maris a long time ago. What had been his problem?

Obviously it was something called stupidity.

Maris hesitated as a fierce wave of nervousness tackled him to the ground. *I should have left my helmet on.* Because right now, for reasons he couldn't fathom, he felt naked and exposed.

Vulnerable.

And he had no idea why.

Worse, he was sure he looked like crap, and he was lucky Ture wasn't cringing in distaste of his sweating grotesqueness. *Please don't let me smell as bad as I fear I do. .* .Though it would serve him right given how many times he'd mocked Darling for his stench whenever his friend had returned from missions.

Suddenly self-conscious, he ran his gloved hand over his hair, hoping to smooth it down and not make it stand up worse.

Really, was there anything uglier than helmet hair?

Uncertain, he went to the cabinet and searched for supplies to stop some of Ture's bleeding. Gathering them together, he forced himself to think about tending wounds and not the fact that Zarya's best friend was absolutely gorgeous. Sexy. Completely edible. . .

Even though Ture had been beaten and tortured, it couldn't take away from his incredible good looks. His reddish brown hair was two shades lighter than Darling's with highlighted tips that had grown out during his imprisonment. As had his beard. Something Maris had never found attractive on any man and yet. . .

Ture made it look good.

Damn good.

Worse, Maris had always been a sucker for a man in pain. It was probably why he'd fallen in love with Darling years ago. The little bugger had taken a beating for him on the first day they met in grade school. That heroic action coupled with the sight of Darling bleeding to protect him had won him over instantly.

But this was very different. Ture wasn't a boy. He was a man full grown and totally delectable. Stupid hormones. Unlike him, they had no loyalty. And they were all standing at attention while he looked down at a man who was as gorgeous as anyone Maris had ever met.

Forcing his thoughts away from the fact that Ture's muscles were well defined and hard, Maris set his supplies on the table next to the bed. He opened the cloth that was soaked in disinfectant then moved back to Ture. "I'm not sure what to give you in way of a painkiller so this is probably going to sting."

"It's fine. Pain I can take."

Brave words. But as Maris set the cloth to the deepest wound on Ture's cheek, he realized the man wasn't bragging. He didn't even flinch.

And that was sexier than hell.

As carefully as he could, Maris cleaned the blood, sweat and dirt from Ture's face so that he could see how bad the injuries were. Yet all he really uncovered was a set of rugged features that did nothing for his sanity. And it didn't help that he knew Ture was definitely on the menu. . .

His gaze burning into him, Ture reached up and covered Maris's hand that was on Ture's cheek with his own. "Thank you."

Ture's gratitude confused him. "For what?"

"Being the man Zarya said you were."

Maris snorted at the compliment that made him deeply uncomfortable. Born and bred in a warrior culture where they had thirty-three words for honor, twenty for loyalty and not a single one for love, Maris could count on one hand the number of times someone had complimented him for anything. "Trust me, I'm more bitch than hero."

Ture laughed then winced as if pain cut through him.

The door opened. Maris turned to see Syn coming in with his helmet off. The Ritadarion thief and assassin was almost even to his height. Syn had his dark hair pulled back into a ponytail, and the liner Syn routinely wore into battle was smudged a bit around his left eye. "How's he doing?"

Maris stepped back to give him room. "Not a doctor."

"Yeah well, to hear Kip tell it, most days I'm not either."

Maris laughed while Syn started examining the cuts and bruises on Ture's face.

Ture wasn't sure what to make of the newcomer. Not until he reached into a drawer by the bed and pulled out a biotec tablet. "I'm Syn," he said in an even, calm tone as he turned the tablet on and entered a medical code. "And I really am a fully licensed doctor. . .graduated number one in my class." He glanced up at Ture. "I'm assuming you're purely Caronese?"

"I am."

Syn narrowed his gaze on him. "One hundred percent? I don't want to give you something and have a nasty surprise over it."

Since Ture had only gone to local doctors on his home planet, he'd never thought about how hard a job it must be should a hybrid life form come in for treatment. "Yeah. As pure-blooded as anyone can be."

"Okay." Syn reached down into the pocket on the left leg of his battlesuit. "I'm giving you something for pain then I'm going to start a drip. I'm sure you're more than aware of the fact that you're badly dehydrated and malnourished." Once he'd injected Ture, he looked over at Maris. "What about you, bud? Is that your blood all over your uniform?"

"Unfortunately. Bastards ruined it."

Syn ground his teeth. "I can stop the bleeding, but you know I have nothing to give you, right?"

"I wouldn't take it even if you did. Just clean it out and I'll heal." Too tired to move anymore, Maris sat down in the corner chair. "How's Zarya?"

"Better now that I peeled Darling off the ceiling. I swear, I almost tranqed his ass. I would definitely not want to be in your brother's shoes right now. We'll have to ride herd on Darling. . .hard. Otherwise, he's going to do something else really stupid to get to Kyr. But back to your question, they busted her up pretty good. Luckily, she'll be fine in a few days, and the baby she's carrying looks to be unaffected by it all. Gods willing." Syn started the IV.

Ture blinked hard as his vision dimmed. Syn hadn't just given him a painkiller. He'd put something in it to knock him out. He wanted to stay awake, but it was a losing battle. In a matter of seconds, he was sound asleep.

Maris frowned as he saw Ture go limp. "Did you—"

"Yeah. He needed it. Besides, I didn't think you wanted him to witness what I'm about to do to treat you."

Good point. Humans often had a hard time dealing with the oddities of the Phrixians. Darling was one of the few who could understand and tolerate Maris's special health needs.

Syn moved toward the sink. "Take your top off."

Maris purred at his command. "You know, I've been waiting for years to hear that come out of your mouth, baby. Should I remove my pants, too? I'm sure I could muster something down there that might require your immediate, personal attention."

Syn laughed at his teasing invitation. "You're the only man who could say that to me and still keep his best friend attached to his body. You're lucky I love you, Mari."

"I know, brother." Maris opened his battlesuit while Syn ran a bowl of water.

When Syn turned back to face him, he froze. His eyes widened in horror.

Maris started to cover himself then stopped. What was the use? Syn had already seen the horrendous scars that marred his flesh. Why cover up now?

"I had no idea," Syn breathed.

Maris shrugged. "You don't grow up gay in a fiercely heterosexual warrior culture without taking a lot of damage." Not to mention his lovely stint as a political prisoner with their enemies for a full decade. *Thanks, Dad and League, for those atrocious nightmares.* "In spite of what my family says, I'm pretty sure they knew all along, and they went out of their way to beat it out of me."

"Does Darling know?"

Maris shook his head. "I don't get naked around Darling." It was why he always kept himself covered from head to foot. Many times, he even wore gloves. Only his lovers had ever seen his body, and even then he kept the room as dark as possible so that no one knew the full weight of the shame he carried with him.

"If it makes you feel better, Nykyrian and I both have more scars than you do."

And so did Darling.

He looked up at Syn. "For the record, Syn, it doesn't make me feel better to know the people I love best have suffered even more than I have. *Really* doesn't."

Syn placed a comforting hand on his shoulder and gave a light squeeze. "And that's why we love *you*, Mari."

Maris didn't respond as Syn started working on his numerous injuries. He did, however, grimace as the pain intensified. If only he could get to a tub of water. . .

Damn.

"You okay?" Syn asked, his voice tense with concern.

"I'm not going to die. Darling would never forgive me for it."

Syn laughed. "Knowing him, he'd follow you into hell if you did and drag you back out."

"And all of you would be right by his side, battling demons the whole way, in and out."

"Yeah well. . .we're stupid that way."

Yes, they were. And that was why he was devoted to all of them.

Syn stood up and wiped his hands on a clean cloth. "Anything I can get for you?"

Maris shook his head. "Thanks, though."

"You need me, buzz. I'm heading back to Zarya."

Maris pulled his battlesuit back on as Syn left. Then he stood and returned to Ture's side. He couldn't imagine what the two of them had been put through because of his brother's sadistic madness. Guilt stabbed him hard. He shouldn't feel responsible for Kyr's actions and yet he always had.

"I won't let him hurt you anymore," he whispered, brushing his hand through Ture's hair. "I promise."

TURE CAME AWAKE TO THE sensation of someone starting to pick him up. Thinking it was a League soldier, he opened his eyes, ready to fight then relaxed as he met Maris's dark gaze.

Maris released him instantly. "Sorry, love. I didn't mean to startle you."

Ture smiled at Maris's deep, pleasant accent. Sometimes he found it difficult to understand Maris's words. Still, he adored the sound of his lilting cadence. "It's okay. I'd much rather wake up to you than a League guard."

"That's not exactly a compliment since I'm rather sure the devil himself would be preferable to that."

True.

Ture bit his lip as he realized that while he'd slept Maris had combed his hair and freshened up. Damn, he was exquisite.

"Maris? Would it be rude if I asked you where you're from? I know from your accent that you're not Caronese."

"Not rude at all. I'm Phrixian."

"Ah."

Maris gave him a wicked, taunting grin. "You have no idea, do you?"

"Not a clue. In fact, if I had a starchart in front of me, I still wouldn't know where to even start to look for it. I've heard of your people, but really know very little other than the name."

"That is a personal choice." Maris winked at him. "We don't like or trust outsiders so we're not real forthcoming with details about our people or territories."

"Really?"

He nodded. "If you're ready, we docked about ten minutes ago. Zarya wants you taken to the palace with her until Syn clears you, health wise. She said you don't have anyone at home to watch over you."

"I would argue, but she's right." The only person in his apartment was Anachelle, and he was taking care of her. She was in no shape to watch over him as he healed.

When he started to get up, Maris stopped him. He indicated the machine pole next to the bed. "You're still attached, love."

Syn reentered the room. "How's he doing?"

"Not the doctor."

Syn rolled his eyes at Ture over Maris's words. "He always says that."

Maris held his hands up in a very feminine and adorable gesture. "Hey, I respect expertise and when it comes to health, I know nothing. Especially not about other races."

Without a word, Syn detached the bed from the wall so that it could be used as a stretcher. He put the fluid bag onto a smaller pole that was near Ture's head. "You coming?" he asked Maris.

"Right behind you, precious."

Ture felt awkward being wheeled into Darling's palace.

While he'd seen the royal abode thousands of times in his life and had toured the public governing sections as part of a school trip decades ago, he'd never dreamed of seeing the private areas.

They went in through a rear entrance, and toward an elevator. The staff turned to look at them, but no one said anything or stopped them. Syn took him upstairs to a room where servants were quickly preparing it.

Ture's jaw dropped at the luxury. He'd never seen anything finer. The ceiling over his head held elaborate gold trim and was painted with a breathtaking celestial scene. It was like looking up at heaven.

The bed was larger than Ture's entire bedroom. . .okay, a slight exaggeration. Still, it was giant. The bed held a navy blue canopy that was trimmed in gold and maroon—the royal Caronese colors.

The door opened.

Ture half expected it to be a guard telling them to get out. So when he saw Darling, the royal governor, coming into the room to check on him, he was stunned.

"How is he?"

Syn moved him to the bed. "Pretty busted up. Broken arm and shin. Severe hand trauma, but we should be able to get him up and running in a few weeks. I called in a friend of mine to do surgery on his hand. He should regain at least ninety percent usage."

"Ninety?" Ture gasped.

"Sorry. . .you might have full recovery. I'm not an expert, which is why I'm calling in a favor from my friend who is. He'll be able to give you a better prognosis than I can."

Ture wanted to scream in aggravation. "How much will all of this cost me?"

"Nothing," Darling said. "I'll cover every bit of it."

His offer offended Ture. "That's not necessary."

"You protected my wife. Zarya said she wouldn't have made it through, but for you. I can't do enough to repay you for that favor. You need *anything*, you let me know."

Maris gasped in outrage of Darling's words. Hands on hips, he sputtered at Darling before he spoke. "You married Lady Z without me? You beast! I'm so heartbroken. How could you? I was supposed to be her maid of honor." He gave an adorable fake pout.

Closing the distance between them, Darling pulled Maris into a tight hug. "You were there in spirit. Besides it was so quick, we were married before we made it to my bedroom."

Ture arched his brow. "You really weren't kidding."

Darling shook his head. "As I told Kyr, the priest was waiting inside the door and started the formalities the instant we entered. I came too close to losing her. Be damned if I'll ever let that happen again."

Ture was still amazed and stunned by the men in this room. That they were everything Zarya had promised him.

Darling kissed Maris's cheek. "Let me know if either of you need anything at all. I'm heading back to Zarya to make sure she doesn't lift anything heavier than a spoon."

Maris laughed. "Good luck with that."

Darling gave a heavy sigh. "I know, right?" Then he left them alone.

"I'm going to get cleaned up and will be back in a few." Maris went to a separate door than the one Darling had used. Rather this one was in the middle of the wall and led to a connecting bedroom.

Ture wasn't sure if he should be flattered or insulted that Maris's bedroom connected to his. Did Maris think him some whore to be kept like a pet?

Syn tucked the covers in around him, and then checked his fluids. "Sorry about the confidentiality breach. But—"

"Darling is technically *the* government. Not like he couldn't have found out anyway."

"There is that." Syn made sure he was comfortable and rechecked all the bandages and medication. Then, he handed Ture a buzzer. "Should you need anything, press that."

"Thank you."

Syn gave a curt nod before he left the room.

Alone, Ture wasn't sure what to make of all this. In all honesty, it scared him. People weren't kind as a rule, and they were cruel to him in particular. *That* he expected.

Even though he appeared to be safe, there was a part of him waiting for this to be some kind of sick joke. He wouldn't put anything past an emperor who'd ascended the throne by viciously assassinating his uncle, and one whose last name was Cruel.

Chapter 2

Ture woke up at the sound of a light knock. "Enter."

Dressed in brown pants and a bright green leather jacket, Maris came into the room carrying a tray in his hands. The instant he stepped inside, the lights turned on to a dim glow. He moved to set it down on the table by the bed. "I know Syn has you hooked up, but thought you might like something tasty to eat and drink."

Ture ground his teeth as he pushed himself up. He was still in a great deal of pain. "Thank you. How long have I slept?"

"Two days."

Ture gasped. With the heavy drapes closed, he couldn't tell if it was day or night outside. "What time is it?"

"Early evening."

He couldn't believe it. "I had no idea."

Maris poured him a cup of hot chocolate then added a bit of cream. "Don't worry. Syn, Darling, Zarya and I both have been checking in from time to time to make sure you were all right."

Ture took the cup from his hands. "That's actually disturbing to know all of you have been in here and I haven't been the wiser."

Maris gave him a devilish grin. "Did you know that you are absolutely gorgeous when you sleep? And you have the lightest little snore. It's actually quite adorable."

Heat crept over his face as those dark eyes teased him with humor. No matter how you cut it, Maris was the sexiest man he'd ever seen. There was so much magnetism to him.

Such an intriguing blend of boyish charm and lethal predator. Most of the time, Maris was relaxed and exuberant. Yet even so, he was always searching with his gaze as if to reassure himself that no assassin had crept in. And he definitely had a warrior's lope.

Head down, gaze intent.

Something Ture's body reacted to with an embarrassing intensity. Lifting his knee slightly to disguise his interest, Ture cleared his throat. "So what food did you bring?"

"An assortment of sandwiches. Since I didn't know what you liked, I thought it the best compromise." Maris pulled the silver lid from the plate and held it out to Ture.

A shudder went through Ture as he accidentally brushed his hand against Maris's. He refused to let Maris know how aroused he was at his mere presence. No good could come of that. "This is more than I can eat. Would you like to share?"

Maris wrinkled his nose playfully. "Sugar, I never pass on food. My mother used to say that I came out of her starving, and practically assaulted the doctor who delivered me to get a bottle from him."

"Really?"

Maris nodded as he daintily picked up one of the small sandwiches and took a bite.

The way Maris savored the food made Ture smile. "You do know what I do for a living, don't you?"

"Not a clue. Zarya never told me."

Ture swallowed his bite. "I'm a chef."

He arched an intrigued brow. "Seriously?"

Ture nodded.

His dark eyes danced with happiness as he slid onto the bed beside Ture. "Ooo, sugar. . .wherever do you work?"

"Angericos on Fifth, downtown."

Maris gasped. "That's *you*? I love that place. Eat there all the time. . .at least when I can get a reservation. Your restaurant is always booked. Even Darling has trouble getting in."

Ture blushed at the compliments. "I try my best not to suck at my job."

"Baby, you succeed admirably." Maris reached for a napkin as the door opened to admit Syn.

He pulled up short at the sight of them together. Then he narrowed a grimace at Maris. "Did you wake him?"

"If I say yes, will you spank me?"

Syn rolled his eyes. "You are terrible, Mari."

Maris scooted off the bed to make room for Syn to check Ture's vitals. "Can't help it. I had too many brothers to annoy. Now it's just hardwired into me to be a major bitch."

Ture frowned. He knew one of Maris's brothers much better than he wanted to. "How many brothers do you have?"

"Eight. Would you like one? I've been trying to give a couple of them away for years now."

He ignored the question. "Any sisters?"

"No. The gods decided not to be so cruel as to throw a girl into that den of testosterone. Then again, maybe they did. *I* was born into it, after all."

Unsure as to what to say to that, Ture met Syn's dark gaze. "How about you?"

"I had a sister. She died a long time ago."

"I'm sorry, Syn. I lost mine, too, when I was a teen. I still miss her."

Syn patted his shoulder. "I'm sorry for your loss, too."

Awkward silence filled the room until Syn finished his review. "You're making good progress. Tomorrow, we need to get you up and moving. I'll schedule a physical therapist for the afternoon. And my surgeon friend will be by day after tomorrow to look over your hand. I've already sent him the scans. He thinks you'll have a full recovery."

Ture felt a rush of excitement at those words. "Thank you, Syn. Seriously."

"No problem. Now you two stay out of trouble and rest for tonight." He turned toward Maris. "And that means you, Mari. I know you haven't slept for two days and you're still healing, too."

Maris gave him a very sarcastic military salute.

Syn ignored it and left them.

"You haven't slept?"

Maris looked away. He started not to answer—that was his standard mode of operation around others—but for some reason the truth came out before he could stop it. "I don't sleep well on my best days. And battle always brings out the worst in me."

"How so?"

Memories surged with a vicious bite as he relived battles he wished to the gods he'd never fought. It was hard knowing the beast that lived inside him—knowing what he was capable of when pushed into a corner. Nothing made him sicker than some of the things war and his family had forced him to do in his past. "Have you ever killed anyone?"

Ture shook his head.

"It's not like you see in movies or programs. It's gory and scary. Disgusting and horrifying. Seeing the look on their faces and in their eyes that moment when they realize their life is over. . .And every time you send someone to their grave, a part of you goes with them."

"Then why do you do it?"

Maris felt his throat tighten. "I stopped fighting for myself a long time ago. But as much as I despise killing, I hate losing someone I love a lot more. How, with all my training and skills, can I stand back and let the ones I love most risk or lose their lives and do nothing for them?"

Ture nodded sympathetically. "I get it. So how old were you the first time you killed someone?"

Maris flinched at the horror of *that* nightmare. "Seventeen."

Ture gaped at the age. "You were a child."

"Not on Phrixus. I was in my second year of obligatory military service."

"It was a battle then?"

He shook his head. "Phrixians are not like other races. We have a very screwed up system of government. And one of the things that greatly differentiates us from others—we have no police force."

"I don't understand. Who enforces the law?"

"The citizens. My people believe that if you can't defend yourself and those who fall under your protection then we don't need your DNA in our gene pool. We take survival of the fittest to its extreme. But that being said, we mostly leave each other alone because we know how highly trained and armed everyone is. The only time someone is attacked is when they're seen as weak."

Ture scowled as he tried to understand the terrifying world Maris described. "You were attacked?"

"My younger brother. I was late picking him up for my father."

Ture winced at the pain he heard in Maris's voice. "Thank the gods you were there."

Maris let out a bitter laugh. "Yeah, but that was the reason he was attacked in the first place."

"You've lost me again."

There was so much agony in those dark eyes that it made Ture's tear up for him. "They thought my brother was me since they'd been told that was where I'd be at that designated time. Had I been on time, my brother wouldn't have been beat to a pulp."

His jaw went slack. It would be hard enough to have your brother attacked. To then find out it was supposed to be you. . .How awful. "Why did they go after you?"

"Swabbing the gene pool." Maris looked away as he remembered the laughter and mockery that had been shoved down his throat.

"You're a pathetic waste. I should have cut out your heart when you were born, instead of wasting family resources on you." Maris could still see the hatred in his father's eyes as he'd sneered that at him.

He met Ture's gaze and tried to keep the bitterness from his voice. "It'd gotten out that I'd had trouble sustaining an erection in a whorehouse with a woman. And such a thing is considered shameful and considered a grave mark against my family and their honor."

"You're kidding."

Maris shook his head. "Erectile dysfunction is deemed a capital offense in our empire."

Ture was appalled by what he described. "They would really kill someone for that?"

Maris nodded. "By the time I arrived, my little brother was barely alive from their vicious assault. The fury inside me was terrifying. And I unleashed every ounce of it onto the three hulking men who were standing over him. I didn't even realize what I'd done until they were in pieces on the ground and I was vomiting against the wall."

Ture took his hand into his and held it tight. "I am so sorry. I can't believe anyone would do such a thing for such a stupid reason. Who sent them after you?"

My father. Maris tightened his hand around Ture's as the answer echoed in his head. To this day, he couldn't bring himself to say that out loud. It was something he'd never told a single soul.

Not even Darling.

The saddest part? His father had bragged about it to Maris when he'd returned home, carrying an almost dead Safir in his arms.

A smile had spread across his father's face as he saw them. *"I've never been prouder of you, boy. Here we all thought we'd be burying a defective woman in an unmarked grave tonight. Instead, you've come home redeemed and wearing the blood of three of my best soldiers. Good job, Maris. You've restored our honor."*

It was the only time in his life his father had praised him. But what had sickened him even more was the fact that his father hadn't cared that he put Safir in danger. Barely more than a child, Safir was considered collateral damage to their father and family.

Just like him.

Sighing, he did his best to bury that memory. "It doesn't matter. Three men were dead over something ridiculous."

Ture pulled him into his arms and held him. "I'm sorry, Mari. But I'm glad you're still here."

Maris patted him on the back. "Some days, I am, too." Closing his eyes, he breathed in the scent of Ture's warm body. He might have gone soft on the female whore who'd ratted him out to his father, but that was definitely not his problem right now.

Ture set him on fire.

And all that did was remind him why his body was rife with such demanding need. He hadn't been with anyone in over two years. First had been his need to find Darling after the Caronese Resistance had taken him captive. Nothing else had mattered during the months they'd searched. And sex had been the last thing on his mind. Then, Darling had been found in a condition that made both Ture's and Zarya's combined look like a picnic. The torture and humiliation Darling had suffered at the hands of people who'd been his allies had left him psychotic.

Maris had been so occupied with saving Darling's life and sanity that he'd forgone any other need. Besides, it didn't matter. He was in love with Darling and while he might have relationships with other men, they always left him feeling hollow.

Those men weren't Darling.

Yet as he held Ture, that old need to be in love with someone who could physically love him back surged. Just once in his life, he wanted to go to bed with someone whose happiness meant more to him than his own. He would give anything if he could feel toward a lover one tenth of what he felt for Darling.

Just for one heartbeat.

But it wasn't meant to be.

He'd accepted that a long time ago. Darling would always be heterosexual. Nothing would ever change that, and his best friend would die before sleeping with him.

Why can't I walk away from Darling?

Honestly, he'd tried. He'd gone from one man to another, hoping, aching that one of them would find a way into his jaded heart.

And every one of them had disappointed him, and left him with scars that were deeper and uglier than the ones marring his body.

But as he breathed Ture in, that part of him that he hated most surged forward. Hope was a fickle whore, and he hated the fact that he was her bitch.

You've walked this path a million times, Mari.

Only Darling was Darling. Everyone else was a poor substitution.

Clenching his teeth against the wave of pain, Maris pulled back and got up. He wouldn't mourn something he couldn't change. Forget hope.

He was, and would forever be, Darling's bitch.

Ture scowled as he watched Maris clean up the food he'd brought. There was a darkness to him now that Ture didn't understand. A thick wall of sadness.

Zarya's stories of Maris went through his head. Like him, Zarya didn't trust easily. She was extremely suspicious and cautious.

Yet Maris had won her over with little effort. She idolized this man. Originally, Ture had dismissed all her stories as hero worship and delusions. He'd never dreamed that a man like Maris actually existed.

A king among princes.

Someone who wouldn't hesitate to protect what he loved. A man capable of putting the needs of others above his own. Such beasts were as rare as the fabled iksen that was said to only come out of its cave once every thousand years.

Now that Ture had found one, he wanted to hold on to it for awhile. But even as that thought went through him, he knew the truth.

Love never lasted. People betrayed. And lovers inevitably disappointed each other.

What if they didn't?

Ture tried to squelch that treacherous thought. He didn't want to have hope. Hope had never been kind to him.

Ever.

Still, he couldn't help but wonder if Maris could ever be as loyal to him as he'd been to Zarya and Darling. If Maris could hold his heart in his hand and not shatter it.

Chapter 3

Maris froze as he heard a knock on the door that connected his room to Ture's. In the last two weeks while Ture had been here, he'd never once knocked. Had something happened?

More frightened by that thought than he should be, he crossed the room and opened the door. Ture stood on the other side, looking gorgeous, but sheepish. "Is something wrong?"

"I can't believe I'm admitting this. . .I can't sleep and I'm lonely."

Maris smiled in understanding. He often suffered from that, too. Before Zarya, he'd always had Darling to console him on those nights. They'd stay up for hours, gaming and joking.

Now, he had Hauk for an opponent, but only so long as Hauk wasn't with a woman. Though lately, Hauk had been in a dry spell that would rival Maris's.

"You want to come in?"

A blush spread over Ture's face.

Maris smiled. "I don't expect you to get naked, hon. We're friends."

He snorted. "I don't have many of those."

"Well, you have one in me." Maris stepped back so that he could enter.

Ture was still hesitant. For the last two weeks, he'd purposefully kept a large distance between him and Maris. He knew better than to be attracted to the friend of a friend, especially one who was as beloved as Maris was to Zarya. If they were to become involved and it didn't work out, it would be awkward for all of them.

That was the last thing he wanted.

But tonight was the anniversary of his sister's death, and he couldn't breathe from the memories and pain of her loss. He just needed something to distract his thoughts for a little while.

Biting his lip, he headed for the small settee that was in the center of Mari's sitting room. "Wow," he breathed, looking around at the elegant and spacious area. "And I thought my room was huge."

Maris smiled. "This is the queen's chambers. Rather fitting, all things considered."

Ture laughed as he sat down. "How did you end up here?"

"When Darling took power, he had me moved from my small room on the guest wing to this one so that I'd be closer to his chambers, which are just down the hall now."

"I'll bet that raised a few eyebrows."

Maris went to the breakfast bar on the far wall and poured him a cup of tea then brought it to him. There was an adorable twinkle in his eyes as he wrinkled his nose. "Still does. Even with him married, half the staff and most of the CDS continue to believe he's really gay and just pretending to be Zarya's husband."

Ture took the cup from his hand. "So if you have the queen's chambers, where does Zarya stay?"

"In Darling's room. Before the League kidnapped you two, he was bad about letting her out of his sight. Now. . .I'm not sure he allows her to go to the bathroom without him."

"Yes, but I like that about him."

Maris sat down on the other side of the coffee table, on a comfortable stuffed chair. He reached for his own cup of tea. "Do you want to talk about what's on your mind?"

Ture glanced away as he felt tears pricking his eyes. "My little sister died of cancer when I was a teen, and. . ." He broke off, unable to finish the sentence. "I still can't believe she's gone."

Maris moved to kneel next to him. He placed a kind hand on Ture's knee. "I'm very sorry."

Ture swallowed against the painful lump in his throat. "It's so hard, you know? She was the only member of my family who really loved me. The only one who didn't judge me."

"Was she your only sibling?"

"No, I have an asshole brother who comes around whenever he needs a favor or money."

Maris scoffed. "Asshole brothers I know a lot about."

"Yeah, I'll bet you do. Do any of them ever contact you?"

"Safir. But it's very dangerous for him to do it. I'm lucky he loves me enough to be stupid."

Ture laughed. "I adore the way you describe things. It's unique."

Maris winked at him. "Far be it from me to ever be normal. I don't like doing what's expected of me." He gave a squeeze to Ture's knee then returned to his chair and tea. "What about you?"

"Definitely not normal."

"Normality is overrated."

"Some day's so is sanity."

Maris laughed. "I couldn't agree more."

Ture stirred cream into his tea as he watched the elegant way Maris moved. He held so much grace and dignity. Regal refinement bled from every part of him and at times it left Ture feeling inadequate. Like a bumbling hick. Yet Maris never seemed to mind the fact that he was lowborn. "So what's it like being a prince?"

"It's no different from any other life, except you have to watch your back more carefully. Enemies and desperate news reporters abound. It makes one extremely paranoid."

"You seem to handle it well."

"Mostly because I don't care. What are they going to do to me? Call me names? Oh, the horror! Someone save me from hearing the opinion of someone I couldn't care less about."

Ture shook his head. "I respect that about you. I hate to be criticized. It's like a knife in my heart."

Maris toyed with the handle on his cup. "I guess it comes from my childhood where I was insulted so much that I honestly thought my name was Idiot and Dumbass."

"You did not."

"Oh, I assure, I did. Darling is the only one who ever called me by name."

"I'm sorry, Mari."

He shrugged with a nonchalance that Ture was beginning to suspect was a front. "Nothing for you to be sorry over. We all have our burdens. Just some of us have the ones that strive to kill us vindictively."

"You joke about things that floor me."

"Yes, well, I tried seriousness once and found it made my butt look fat. Who wants to live like that?"

In that moment, the urge to kiss Maris was so strong, he wasn't sure how he refrained. All he could think about was peeling off the layers of clothing until he had him naked in his arms. If Maris was one tenth as animated in bed as he was in casual conversation, he'd be an incredible lover.

Maris's link buzzed. He pulled it out and checked it then smiled. "Please excuse me for a second." He flipped it open. "Hey, Hauk. How's my luscious Andarion tonight?"

Ture swallowed against the weird stab of jealousy that he couldn't fathom. He had no right to be possessive of Maris, and yet. . .

He wanted to have the right to complain when Mari flirted with other men.

"No, sweetie. I actually have company tonight." Maris laughed. "You keep talking to me like that and you'll have more of me than you can handle."

Feeling suddenly awkward, Ture was about to excuse himself when Maris ended the call.

"Sure. I'll talk to you later." He hung up.

Ture knew he should keep his mouth shut, but he couldn't resist asking the one question foremost on his mind. "Boyfriend?"

Maris flashed him an adorable grin. "You can stop asking me that. I don't have one and have no interest in being tied down to any one man."

That stung like a slap. "Ah. You're one of *those*."

Maris arched a brow. "Those?"

"Players."

Maris laughed so hard, he choked. "Hardly. I assure you, I never play the field. My only problem is the man I love is currently in bed with *your* best friend."

"Darling?"

He nodded.

"So you and he—"

"Have *never* touched."

"Not even a kiss?"

"Not even." Maris sighed. "I am forever drawn to what I can't have. It's extremely irritating."

Ture knew the feeling. "You think you'll ever find someone?"

"Honestly? I stopped looking. There's only so many dreams a man can have shattered in one lifetime. I think I exceeded my quota when I was three." Maris took a sip of his tea. "What about you?"

"My work is my love. No man has ever been as seductive or as rewarding. It's the only thing worth my time."

"So you love your kitchen."

Ture nodded. "I'm as married to it as Zarya is to Darling. It's where I spend almost all my waking hours."

"Are you nervous about having been gone from it for so long?"

"I was. But Anachelle said that she's been staying on top of everything for me while I've been away."

"Anachelle?"

Ture smiled. "Like Zarya, I rather adopted her. She was a waitress in the restaurant where I work and when she became pregnant, she lost everything. So I offered her a bed and she's been with me for the last few months."

Maris was impressed with his kindness. "What made you trust her?"

"If you ever meet her, you'll understand. She's a lot like Zarya. Guarded and wounded. Yet there's a hope inside her that all her hardships have yet to extinguish. Not to mention, she's precious and kind."

"I like her already." Maris got up to refresh their teas then returned to converse with Ture until the sun came up.

Yawning, Maris gaped as he realized what time it was. He couldn't remember the last time he'd stayed up all night talking to anyone.

Even Darling.

"Did you know it's seven already?"

Ture's jaw dropped as he turned to look at the windows. "Where did the night go?"

"It turned into daylight."

Ture duplicated Maris's yawn. "No wonder I'm so tired." Getting up, he groaned.

"Are you all right?"

Yawning again, Ture nodded. They had spent the entire night talking about everything and nothing. Maris had definitely kept his promise to distract Ture's thoughts from his sister. "Thank you, Mari."

He inclined his head to him. "Any time."

Ture kissed his cheek then he headed to his own room.

Maris didn't move as his cheek tingled from those lips. Lips he wanted to taste with a madness that made no sense.

Why am I always attracted to what I can't have?

And he had no idea what it was about Ture that

fascinated him so. Well, not entirely true. There was something about him that Maris found easy to talk to. He didn't feel like Ture judged him. Rather he seemed to be fine with all of Maris's quirks.

It was enough to make him reconsider his vow of solitude. But dreams were for fools.

And Maris was through being hurt.

Chapter 4

"PUSH YOURSELF HARDER."

Ture paused, mid stroke to glare at Maris as he coached him from the side of the large pool deep inside the Caronese Winter Palace where he was still recuperating. "I'm pushing as hard as I can. If you think you can do better, I defy you to crawl in here and try."

Maris flashed a charming smile at him. "I'd hate to show you up, love. This is about your progress, not my greatness."

Unamused, Ture rolled his eyes at the pomposity. That was the one thing that could get irritating about Maris. His ego was as vast as the universe. But Ture also knew it was a front. For all his bluster, Maris was actually quite insecure and bashful. Preciously so at times.

For almost a month now, Ture had been in physical therapy as his body healed, and he learned to use it again and rebuild atrophied muscles. Oddly, these sessions seemed to be getting harder instead of easier.

And right now. . .

Ture gasped as his leg locked up. Because he had so little body fat, he sank to the bottom of the pool like an anchor. He tried to swim up, but couldn't get his body to cooperate. His heart pounding, he knew that Maris couldn't swim. It was why he'd never joined him for any of the water exercises.

If he didn't get to the surface. . .

He panicked even more.

All of a sudden, someone grabbed him from behind and pulled him up.

Ture coughed and choked as they broke the surface. He glanced around for Maris. His jacket and shirt were where he'd been, but there was no sign of him.

At least not until the man holding him lifted him out of the water with an ease that was terrifying.

Maris?

Still choking, he turned back toward the pool.

"Don't look at me," Maris growled. He held himself below the edge of the pool so that all Ture could see was his hand.

A hand that now held a strange translucent silver color and long fingernails that were more claw-like than Maris's flawless manicure. . .

"Mari?"

"I'm all right, Ture. Just don't look at me."

But he couldn't help himself. His curiosity was too great. Before he could think better of it, he inched his way toward Maris and peeped over the edge. His eyes widened at what he found in the water.

Gasping, he stumbled back as raw fear gripped him. What the hell?

Maris flinched at the look he'd seen on Ture's face. With the exception of Darling, humans didn't handle seeing Phrixians in their natural state gracefully. Who could blame them? His species was repugnant.

Oh well. . .it wasn't like there could ever be anything between them anyway.

Suddenly, Ture was back at the edge, leaning over it. His eyes guarded, he reached down to touch Maris's wet hair.

"I know," Maris sighed. "I'm disgusting."

"No. You're very beautiful like this."

Stunned, Maris looked up, unsure of what to expect. But he saw truth in Ture's eyes, not horror.

Ture cupped Maris's cheek as he stared in awe of the man's current appearance. He'd never seen anything like this. Mari's skin reminded him of a sleek, silvery fish's. Only it wasn't scaled and it was as soft was warm velvet. Even his eyes were now an eerie glowing silver color. Not their normal dark chocolate. The neatest part was the beautiful design that was now visible around his eyes. Like someone had used dark gray and black eye shadow and liner to draw an intricate flowing scroll pattern.

He placed his hand over Maris's as he studied its differences, too. His nails were a bit longer, coming just over the end of his fingers, and he now had webbing between the phalanges. "Do your feet do this, too?"

Maris nodded. "So that we can grip better in wet environments." He pressed one nail deep into the concrete with almost no effort and no effect on his finger, but there was a deep line furrowed in its wake as he dragged it back toward him. "We're amphibious. But we're much stronger in the water than on land. It's what makes my people such lethal assassins. If we can get our target in the water, we own them and nothing can stop us."

That was terrifying to think about. "Why didn't you tell me?"

Maris looked away. "We're not supposed to let anyone outside of our own know. Ever. On Phrixus, I'd be killed for this."

Ture gaped at him. "You'd have let me die?"

He flashed a wicked grin. "On Phrixus. . .yes."

Laughing at something he knew Maris wouldn't really do, Ture shook his head. His gaze fell to Maris's well-sculpted wet body. While he'd suspected how finely toned it was, he'd never seen it before. Not even a glimpse. For all his flamboyance, Mari always kept himself completely covered from neck to feet and all the way to his wrists.

Now Ture knew why. Maris's back was a nasty roadmap of scars. Scars that ran down his arms and over his chest. Without thinking, Ture reached down to touch one that had barely missed Maris's heart. "What happened?"

"I was a soldier with a lot of battle experience." Maris covered Ture's hand with his. "That one is a present from my older brother once he found out I was gay and tried to kill me for the dishonor I'd done to my family."

Ture winced at words that cut through his own heart and reminded him how badly his own parents had reacted. Though to be honest, none had tried to kill him for it. "I'm sorry."

Maris shrugged as he released Ture's hand. "It is what it is. If everyone was decent, how could we legitimately fight each other? Assholes keep us sharp."

A sad smile curved his lips as he watched the ease with which Maris treaded water. "You seem to be enjoying that pool."

"I told you, we're amphibious, and are born underwater. It's our most natural environment. We don't really walk land until we're almost in school."

"Really? And here I thought you avoided the water because you couldn't swim."

Maris laughed. "Hardly. I didn't venture onto land until I was five."

"Do you remember it?"

A dark shadow fell across his eyes, letting Ture know it was a painful memory. "I do." Shaking it off, Maris held his hand out to Ture. "Want to join me?"

Ture's gaze dropped to the dark pants Maris was still wearing. "You're going to swim half dressed?"

"We don't swim naked at home. It tends to be frowned upon. Phrixians are lethal, yet civilized. Of course, our clothes are water resistant, but I'm used to this, too. It doesn't bother me in the least."

Ture returned to the pool.

Amazed, he studied Maris as he headed straight to the

bottom to swim for several minutes. He was fascinating to watch. Mari twisted and turned in ways Ture wouldn't have thought anyone with a spine could manage. But what was really shocking was how much speed he had. He could shoot from one end of the enormous pool to the other so fast that Ture could barely follow it with his eyes.

Maris was truly a thing of beauty. And full of pleasant surprises that intrigued him a lot more than they should.

Don't go there.

He knew better than to get involved with the friend of a friend. It never worked out. Ever. And still he couldn't keep from seeing Maris as the most desirable thing on two legs. Something helped by the fact that Maris seemed to feel the same way about him. Yet Maris kept his distance.

Another thing that was sexy as hell. He had integrity where most people didn't.

Maris shot up in the water, a few feet from him with a smile on his face that made Ture really glad he was in the water. Otherwise, Maris would know exactly how lickable he found him.

"It feels so good," Maris breathed. "You've no idea how hard it's been watching over your therapy while dying to jump in. Water is like the air we breathe." He sank down so that all Ture could see was that incredible set of eyes.

"I can tell. I don't think I've ever seen you this animated."

Maris sobered instantly.

Ture frowned at his reaction. "Did I hit a nerve?"

Maris raked his hands through his wet hair. Damn. . . he had the most perfect features of any man Ture had ever seen.

"Ghosts. Sorry. I try to keep them hidden, but sometimes they pop out at the worst times."

Ture swam closer to him. "Yeah, I know all about those."

Maris swallowed as Ture touched his shoulder in sympathy. The heat of his hand combined with the look on Ture's face held him immobile. He knew he should pull back. Yet he couldn't get his body to cooperate.

Not when all he really wanted to do was swim closer.

Before he could move, Ture captured his lips with his own. Maris growled at the sweet taste of him. It'd been way too long since he'd been this close to anyone except Darling. Every hormone in his body went into overdrive, and it was all he could do not to show Ture exactly how limber and powerful he was in water.

His breathing labored, Maris nipped Ture's chin as long-buried fantasies about having sex in the water surged. Since his people killed anyone who wasn't heterosexual and he'd never dared to let anyone know about this side of him, he'd only been naked with a lover in water in his dreams.

But now. . .

Don't go there.

Ture couldn't breathe as he felt the full power of Maris in his arms. Somehow, Maris managed to hold them both steady in the water.

For as long back as Ture could remember, he'd dreamed of having a hot, masculine warrior of his own. But never had he thought to meet one who could be so incredibly skilled in war and yet tender to others. All his past soldiers had been as vicious to him as they'd been to their victims. Maris was the strangest dichotomy of brutal killer and playful charmer. At times, it was like two men inhabited his lush body.

And Ture found both of them delectable.

Maris deepened the kiss then pulled back. His breathing heavy, he skimmed Ture with a look that only made him hungrier. "We can't do this."

Ture pressed his cheek to Maris's. "I know, sweetie. I'm sorry. . .I couldn't resist you." He placed a chaste kiss to him then moved away.

Maris ground his teeth as he watched Ture return to his physical therapy routine. The fact that Ture understood and agreed made him all the more alluring. It was rare to find someone who was willing to put the needs of others above their own. That was the heart and soul of Darling that had kept Maris bound to him all these years. Why he'd never been able to walk away from his best friend even when he knew he should.

Because that was his life's blood, too. He would never fight for himself. He couldn't care less what happened to him. He only fought for who and what he loved.

Darling, above all others, for the simple fact that Darling had bled for him on more than one occasion.

The rest was a short list made up of the only brother Maris had who still spoke to him—Safir, Darling's immediate family, the Sentella and Caillen Dagan.

Now Ture stood to inherit that small circle. But not if he broke Maris's heart. And though he would give anything to let Ture in, he knew better. He'd been down this bloody path too many times. As soon as his lovers realized that they could never supplant Darling in his heart, they turned on him with a justified hatred.

Maris couldn't help how he felt. Darling owned him. He always had. Even though they could and would never be anything more than best friends, Darling was his heart. He'd been there for Maris when no one else had. When the entire universe had slammed down on him and no one had cared, Darling, alone, had traversed hell itself to save Maris's life.

He shuttered every time he thought of where he'd be without his noble prince. If he'd even be alive.

Sighing, he lifted himself out of the water to sit on the edge of the pool while Ture continued swimming. Memories surged as he reached for a towel. Even now, he could see Darling the day they'd met as tiny kids on a playground.

Because of his young age, Maris had been cloistered on Phrixus and hadn't fully learned the Universal language. For that matter, he'd barely known how to walk. One day, he'd been a caudate, learning about his own people and laws, and the next he'd been ripped out of his world and sent to exist among humans and their strange, foreign rules. Rules that had baffled and scared him.

His father's only dictate for behavior had been harsh. *Shame or betray us and I'll cut out your heart myself and feed it to you before you die. One word that you've violated any human code or custom, and you will be put down for it.*

The man had not been joking or exaggerating.

Barely five years old, Maris had been terrified of making a single mistake.

And even now, all these years later, he saw Lord Trustan's beady eyes as he'd given Maris his new code of conduct. *You so much as breathe on one of our children, or do any act of violence against any human and you will be sent home to your father in pieces. Understood?*

The moment Trustan had said those words, his own sons had known Maris was fair game for their abuse.

And they'd bled him well for no other reason than his people had been at war with theirs for centuries.

By the time school had started, Maris had been a well-used doormat who hadn't dared to fight back for fear of what his family would do for the "dishonor," or Trustan either, for that matter.

Trustan's eldest son, Crispin, had been the one who'd chased him across the schoolyard that fateful day. While Maris hadn't really understood the insults they'd yelled, he knew the misery of being punched and slapped while being unable to strike back.

Tired of it all, he'd been praying for death when out of nowhere a boy half his size had slammed into Crispin and knocked him away from Maris.

Like some mythical hero, Darling had beat the bastard down and told him that he better never touch Maris again. Then he'd turned around, bleeding and bruised, and extended his hand to Maris. "Hi, I'm Darling Cruel. We should be friends." In that heartbeat, Maris had fallen head over heels in love with him. And he'd been that way ever since.

He'd never met anyone who came close to Darling's loyalty, kindness, or generous spirit.

Until Ture.

For Zarya, he'd put his life on the line without hesitation. A woman who wasn't family, but a friend he'd loved and placed above himself. There weren't many people who would do such a thing for anyone.

It didn't hurt that Ture had one of the hottest bodies he'd seen in awhile, too. Best of all, Ture hadn't freaked out over Maris's "uniqueness."

Ture swam over to him and boldly put his hand on the edge of the pool, right between Maris's slightly parted thighs. "Can I call it a day yet?"

It wasn't easy to understand those words as a fantasy went through his mind and left his brain devoid of all blood flow. "Um, yeah."

Gah, I hope I didn't just promise to buy him something really expensive. . ..

Ture moved away and pulled himself out of the pool next to him. He grabbed a towel and started drying his hair. A handsome mixture of frown and smile came over his face. "It doesn't take you long to change back, does it?"

Maris looked down at his normal "flesh" tone. "No. Within a few minutes of leaving the water, we return to a human appearance."

"What about sweating? Does that turn you?"

Maris shook his head. "It has to be full submersion. The only real danger of accidental exposures are torrential downpours."

Ture took his hand into his and examined it. "That's just so neat. Does it hurt at all when you change?"

"No. We don't even notice, really."

"It must suck, though."

"How so?"

"Unless you're with a Phrixian, you can't shower with your lover."

Maris quirked a smile. "A definite hardship in the past. I've offended several men over it."

Ture pulled him to his feet then hugged him close. "Thank you for saving my life. . .both times."

Maris forced himself to release Ture as he stepped away. His body hard and aching, he watched as Ture went to dress.

Hunger settled deep in his stomach, but he knew better. No good could come of dating Ture. It would be a titanic mistake.

Sighing, Maris had just finished pulling his shirt and jacket on when Darling came into the room. He drew up short as he saw Maris's wet pants.

His jaw slack, he quickly turned to see that Ture was gone. "What happened?"

Maris towel dried his hair. "He almost drowned. I jumped in to save him."

"So Ture knows?"

Maris nodded.

Which caused Darling to frown. "You okay, bud?"

Maris paused as he thought about how to best answer. "Honestly? I don't know. He didn't really react to it. . . which is good, I guess."

Darling cracked a knowing grin. "But bad?"

Maris laughed at Darling's ability to read him so well. "For my sanity, yes. It is terrible."

"Why? He's available. . .You're available."

Not really and that was the problem. His heart only wanted to love one man—Darling. "Yeah, but when we break up, it's going to be rough to have to see him whenever he's with Zarya. I like having boyfriends I can walk away from and never lay eyes on again. You know?"

"Since the only girlfriend I've ever had is my wife, not really. But I respect your decision. I always have."

"And that's why I love you." Maris kissed Darling on his cheek then went to change pants.

But as he left, his thoughts turned to the one thing he'd always wanted yet never had found.

Someone who would be with him forever. That one person who could hold his heart in his hands and not shatter it.

Chapter 5

Maris walked around Ture's bedroom with a lump in his stomach. He'd known in the beginning that as soon as Ture was healed, he'd return home and that he wouldn't see him except for occasional visits with Zarya. And while that had seemed acceptable to him at the time. . .

Now. . .

He really missed him and he'd only been gone for a week. But it was the longest week of Maris's life. Worse, he felt like something was now missing. How sad was that?

I am pathetic.

Honestly, he should leave here and find his own place to live. Darling didn't need him anymore. He had Zarya now and the two of them spent most of their time together. Which was how it should be. A man's spouse should be his primary focus.

But it left Maris terribly lonely. Ture had been a nice distraction for him. They had eaten together and talked about absolutely nothing for hours on end. Watched old movies. . .

Maris sighed wistfully. The only trouble was he had nowhere else to go. He was dead to his family. Because of the species differences and the fact that he was jaded to a frightening level, he didn't really have friends, except for the Sentella who were all married.

Not Hauk.

He smiled at the thought. Hauk was probably the only person who made him look optimistic by comparison. And while he adored the gargantuan Andarion, they were far too different to hang out on a regular basis. Other than gaming and mutual friends, they had nothing in common.

His link buzzed. Maris started to ignore it, but as soon as he looked down, he saw Ture's ID. A smile broke out before he could stop it.

He answered immediately.

Ture cleared his throat. "Hey. . .I um. . .how are you?"

Maris smiled even wider at the hesitancy in Ture's voice. "Fine." *Missing you like crazy.* He caught himself before he said that out loud. Absolutely no good could come from Ture knowing just how much Maris longed for his company. "How are you?"

"Fine."

A sudden awkward silence filled the line as Maris tried to think of something half intelligent to say that wouldn't make him appear like some lovesick idiot. "How's your apartment?"

"Fine."

More awkwardness.

"How's Zarya?" Ture asked.

Maris slipped out of the room and returned to his own. He knew Ture couldn't see him unless he turned on the video feed, but for some reason it felt weird to be in Ture's guestroom while talking to him. "She's very well. Stressed a little from the magnitude of planning a state wedding to ensure the legitimacy of her baby, but. . .she's much better."

"Good."

Maris bit his lip. He had no idea why this was so difficult. They'd never had trouble speaking to each other before and yet—

This sucked.

"So, Mari, I was wondering. . .I know how much you like good food. . ."

He cringed in fear of having to turn Ture down for a date.

"Tonight, the special at my restaurant is Chipped Oryan. Since I know it's one of your favorite dishes and you like eating here, I wanted to let you know. If you're interested, I can hold a table for you. It's our busiest night and I won't be able to say more than a passing hello while you dine, but I have to tell you that I make the best in the Nine Worlds. You will cry to your mother at how good it is, and I'll spoil you from ever eating anyone else's."

Maris laughed at an invitation he couldn't refuse. "Sure," he said before he could stop himself. "I'd love to see if you're half the chef you claim to be."

"Oh, baby, I'm better."

Maris sucked his breath in at the endearment. He didn't know why, but the sound of Ture's accent whenever he was flippant and sweet. . .

It made his mouth water.

"So what time should I tell them to expect you?" Ture asked.

"Eight?"

"Perfect. I'm entering it in right now. They'll have the table all ready for you when you get here. Just give them your name."

"Thanks. I really appreciate it."

"No problem. Later."

Maris cut the transmission then slid the link into his pocket and checked the time.

All right, I have six hours. He'd best start dressing now or he'd be late.

MARIS HESITATED AS HE SAW the long line of people waiting to get into the restaurant where Ture worked. But then it was always like this. He knew from his past visits that Ture was a great chef. So much so that it was almost half an hour just to reach the maitre d' stand.

The man didn't even look up from his e-ledger. "Reservation name?"

"Maris Sulle."

"With an S?"

"Yes."

With a withering snobbiness that would make one of Darling's senators proud, the man glanced over his ledger. "Sorry." Snide overrode pity as he finally glanced up and raked Maris with a haughty curled lip that said he suspected Maris was lying about having a reservation. "There's no Sulle. Is there another name it might be under?"

Maris swallowed as embarrassment filled him, and he hated the man for making him feel it in front of so many people.

Had he mistaken the night? Or had Ture forgotten to add him, after all? "Could you check again?"

The maitre d' raked him with an even snottier sneer. "I am highly literate. . .in multiple languages. Your name is *not* here."

Maris went into his own round of military peerage snobbery. The one thing about his noble and warring family. . .no non aristo *ever* condescended to them.

At least not if he wanted to keep his testicles attached to his body.

"As am I. Perhaps it's under one of my titles. Prince or Ambassador?"

That took the bastard down a bit. "Um. . .no, Highness. I still don't see you listed. Sorry." This time, at least, there was a modicum of sincerity to that word.

"Thank you." Even though he felt extremely bitch-slapped, Maris gathered what little dignity he could and turned to leave.

As he reached the door, someone touched his arm. He turned to find a tiny pregnant woman who barely reached the middle of his chest.

"Are you Maris, my lord?"

Still aware of the smug leering faces of those who'd seen his humiliation, he gave a curt nod.

She let out an exasperated breath. "I knew it when I saw you! You look just like Ture described you. I am so sorry Bertram's a dumb ass. Please, come with me. Ture's asked and asked all night if you were here yet."

With those few words, she made him feel instantly better. "After you, madame."

She smiled and turned to lead him back into the restaurant.

"Excuse me?" Bertram snapped as they started past his station. "Where do you think you're going?"

She glared at him with an artificial smile. "Hopefully to save your job and your stupid ass. Instead of giving me attitude, you should be saying, thank you."

Color suffused his cheeks.

She reached past Bertram to show the handwritten note that was taped to this stand. Jerking it loose, she slapped it against his chest and left it to hang there. "Lord Maris is a personal friend of Ture's, you moron. He'd have chewed your rump for dessert had I not come out of the restroom in time to catch sight of the man he told all of us to keep our eyes open for. Remember the meeting?"

Paling considerably, he looked at the paper then to Maris. "I am so incredibly sorry. I-I-I-"

"Keep sputtering," she said, "then find us when you finally have an intelligent thought again." She turned back to Maris with a friendly, heartfelt smile. "Please, my lord, come with me."

Maris offered her his arm.

She took it and led him into the restaurant and then to his complete confusion, through the double doors and into the commercial kitchen area. Really uncomfortable, he slowed down.

Without a word, she pulled him toward a far corner in the rear where a table was set even nicer than the ones for their clientele. She pulled a padded chair out for him. "My name's Anachelle. What can I get for you to drink, my lord?"

So this was the woman Ture had taken in. As Ture had predicted, Maris understood now why Ture had been so kind to her. Something about her was very kind and sweet, and it wasn't just because she'd gallantly saved his ego. "The dry house wine."

"Very good, my lord. I'll be right back."

Still uncomfortable, Maris assumed his full aristocratic bearing as he noted the number of curious glances he received from the staff as they worked while Ture was nowhere to be seen.

This was really awkward.

Maybe he should have stayed at home. . .

TURE CAME TO A COMPLETE standstill as he left the freezer and finally saw the one face he'd been dying to see for days now. He'd been jittery and nervous since the moment Maris had accepted his invitation.

Now Maris was here. . .

And he was even more handsome than he remembered.

Ture swallowed hard as he admired the way Maris looked. Dressed in an expensive black suit that was a lot more conservative than the man wearing it, Maris was the same rigid military commander who'd rescued him. He bled total masculinity and ferocity. Confidence and elegance.

The word sexy was an understatement when applied to a man like him.

"Mari?"

He turned with full aristocratic bearing and rose slowly to his feet. "Ture." He inclined his head to him.

Confused by his continued stern formality, Ture frowned as he closed the distance between them. "Is something wrong?"

Keeping a respectful and aggravating distance, Maris

leaned down slightly to whisper in his ear. "I don't know how open you are, and I don't want to get you into trouble at work with your boss."

That was the kindest thing anyone had ever said or done for him in his life. And it explained the conservative clothing that hugged his lean, well-muscled body. And now that Ture thought about it, it looked like Maris had borrowed those somber clothes from Darling.

In that one moment, Ture knew he was definitely in love with this man. Even though he barely knew him.

Smiling, he turned his head and captured Maris's lips with his for a tender kiss before Maris pulled away. "They all know where my taste lies, sweetie. As for the other? I own the restaurant and while I stay pissed at myself for multitudinous reasons, you're definitely not one of them."

Maris returned his smile and noticeably relaxed. "Oh. Sorry. I didn't mean to insult you or presume anything. The way you talk about it, I thought you just worked here."

It was true. He did. "Force of habit. I started as a cook and bought it from the former owner three years ago."

"Ah."

Anachelle returned with his wine and set it down.

Ture frowned at her. "What did I tell you, missy?"

She drew back with a guilty look. "I had to go to the bathroom. Sorry." She scooted over to the corner where another padded chair was set. "Besides, we're really busy. I should be out there helping."

Maris noted that Anachelle made no mention to Ture about Bertram and what he'd done. It said a lot about her character that she kept that to herself, and didn't seek to harm someone who was obviously unkind by nature.

"And I don't want you to jeopardize that baby. Fold napkins!"

"Yes, sir." Huffing, she dutifully reached for the cart beside her and pulled a burgundy napkin down so that she could turn it into an intricate star shape. She placed it in a plastic container of other like creations.

Maris smiled at Ture's kindness. "I've never seen you bossy before."

"You're not the only one who can be commanding." He wrinkled his nose playfully. "Would you like to see a menu?"

"Your house. Your rules. I'll eat anything other than small children and infants or rodents."

Ture squeezed his arm. "All right. One serving of mystery appetizer coming up."

As Ture headed toward the main cooking area, Maris turned back to Anachelle who watched him curiously. "Is something wrong?"

"No. I like you a lot better than his last boyfriend. He was a total asshole, which is why I think it's been so long since Ture last dated anyone at all. And I mean a l-o-n-g time. You seem very sweet."

Okay. . .He wasn't sure what to make of her or that comment. "I'm not his boyfriend. We're just friends."

"If you say so."

"You don't believe me?"

She reached for another napkin. "I see how you two look at each other. Even from over here, I got a little singed."

Maris didn't know why, but he really liked her. "Here. . ." He moved her chair closer to the table then positioned his so that she could put her feet up on his thigh. "You need to keep them elevated or they'll swell."

She arched a brow at him. "Know a lot of pregnant women, do you?"

"My best friend's wife is expecting so I've done my homework to keep him sane and Zarya from doing something stupid."

Her face lit up at the name. "Zarya Starska?"

"You know her?" Maris asked, surprised by her enthusiasm.

"Oh, I love and adore her! She used to come in and eat all the time. This table was actually put here just for her. . . How is my girl? I haven't seen her in forever. I've missed her so. Is she really pregnant?"

"Fine, and yes."

She laughed at his simple answers to her chaotic rambling. "Well then, it's settled. You must be good people for Zarya to like you. She trusts very few."

"It speaks a lot for you, too." Maris slid her shoes off then sipped his wine in between massaging her feet for her. "When's your baby due?"

"Another month."

"Boy or girl?"

Her smile faded. "Boy."

Maris frowned at her sad tone. "You and his father must be excited."

She clenched her teeth as her eyes darkened with anger. "His father is a married man who ran back to his wife and blocked my calls the moment he found out I was pregnant."

He winced at the cruelty. "Oh, honey, I'm sorry. On behalf of the male species, I would like to thoroughly beat him senseless for being a bastard."

"Thank you, my lord."

"Please, call me Maris or Mari."

Ture approached with an amused expression as he caught sight of her feet in Maris's hands. "Are you two cozy enough?"

Her cheeks pinkened. "Maris did it."

Maris gasped indignantly at her quick exclamation. "Did I just get thrown under a shuttle? I hope someone got the serial number of it."

Smiling, Ture set a plate of cheeses with sauce drizzled over them and a separate plate of crackers. "Not at all. I appreciate your taking care of my girl. Someone needs to."

Anachelle made a sound of supreme annoyance. "He thinks I'm a stray dog. He even took me into his apartment to live until after the baby comes."

"I never thought you were a stray dog, sweets. Just down your luck, which sadly happens to all of us at some point." Ture poured more wine for Maris. Then he indicated the paste in a small bowl on the cracker plate. "That's a pate' with almonds and gixon. If you don't like it, let me know and I can grab you something else."

"It looks and smells delicious."

Ture pulled several small packets out of his pocket for Maris to use to sanitize his hands. "I'm making your Chipped Oryan myself so I better get back to it before it scorches."

As soon as he was gone, Anachelle leaned in to whisper. "It really is the best you'll ever taste, but don't feed Ture's ego. He's arrogant enough about his culinary skills."

As soon as Maris tasted the pate', he understood why. "Oh my God, this is fabulous!" He filled a cracker for Anachelle. "Would you like some?"

"Pregnant and hungry all the time. . .Absolutely. Thank you." She took it from him and reached for her bottled water that was near the napkins. "So what do you do for a living, my. . .Maris."

He smiled at her almost slip. "I'm the Andarion Ambassador for the Caron Empire."

She scowled. "Aren't you supposed to actually be an Andarion for that?"

He laughed at her confusion—which was the typical reaction from everyone he met. "Normally. But the Andarion prince is a good friend of my best friend. He assigned me here before the Grand Counsel's death to ensure the safety of the true royal family."

She went pale. "Your best friend is Darling Cruel? The stupid bastard who just launched us into war against the League?"

Maris steeled himself at words that usually sent him into a murderous frenzy. Just not against pregnant women. "Darling is one of the most intelligent men who's ever been born. A little hot-headed, granted, but never, *ever* stupid. Nor is he cavalier with anyone's life. And I was there when it all happened. The League started this war over Zarya. They wanted to keep her in prison, along with Ture, and a number of other Caronese citizens. Darling is the sole reason any of them are alive today."

"And I will testify to that." Ture set a plate in front of Maris. He spoke to Anachelle. "You know I held no love of the royal family. That definitely changed when Darling, himself, along with Maris came into my prison cell and freed me and Zarya. I know of no other emperor who would have done that for anyone. And he had intended to leave in peace. But the League wouldn't allow him to do that. I stand with our emperor and will do so until the day I die."

Maris arched a brow at Ture's words.

Ture met his gaze. "I never forget blood debts. I've had too many people try to hurt me to squander the decency of anyone who protects my ass." He leaned down to whisper in Maris's ear. "I'm as loyal to friends and family as you are."

Those words, combined with his close proximity, set Maris on fire again.

Ture squeezed his hand then left them so that he could return to work.

Maris turned his attention back to Anachelle.

She held her hands up in surrender. "I trust Ture and as he said, I remember well how often he and Zarya wished much ill on the head of our noble leader. If you can convert them then I'll defer to the three of you. Obviously there's much about the emperor I don't know, and I'm wise enough to know better than to trust the media and their whitewashed lies."

"Good woman. Because Darling is one of the very few people I'd kill or die for." He tasted his food while she went back to folding napkins.

His eyes widened as the savory taste hit him full force. Ture had a definite gift.

"Told you. . ." She beamed with a bright smile. "Ture is a god in the kitchen. It's why they're lined up around the block to get in."

"How does he do it?"

She shrugged. "Stingy thing won't share that info.

But I've seen many men and women, low and highborn, begging him to marry them for his pasta dishes alone."

Amused with her anecdote, Maris watched Ture. He was as fierce and organized as a battle commander as he checked food temperatures, presentation, preparation, and a thousand other things that left Maris's head reeling. It was truly an impressive feat. Ture moved like a dancer in a ballet. Graceful and good-natured. Whenever someone had a problem, Ture moved in to help and had them smiling again. Likewise, he stepped in to settle arguments between his workers. All the while maintaining a jovial temperament.

Truly, truly impressive.

And it was obvious that this restaurant was everything to Ture. It was here he came alive. Happiness shone in his eyes and even though he had to be exhausted, Ture had a light and easy step.

Maris had barely finished his dinner when Ture returned with two lush desserts. One was a chocolate mountain of steaming deliciousness for Maris and a strawberry and cream parfait for Anachelle whose entire face came alight when she saw it.

"I love you, Ture. Marry me!" She laughed as she grabbed a spoon and dug in.

Returning her laugh, Ture kissed her on the cheek. "If I were straight, honey, I would."

She sighed wearily. "Why are all the good men gay or dead?"

"Or married?" Maris asked without thinking. He cringed as she scowled at him and he realized how insensitive it was to say that to *her*. "Sorry. I forgot."

"It's okay. I was the moron who slept with him. Which I would have *never* done had I known he had a wife at home. That's what I get for thinking someone had integrity to not lie about their marital status."

Maris swallowed his food. "Some of us do."

"Yeah, but not enough."

He held his wine glass up to her. "I will heartily agree. I've had my heart carved out enough times to know whereof you speak."

"Yes. . .men suck."

"But not all." Maris winked at her.

"Present company and food gods who bring me sweets are always excluded." She dug in again with a gleeful greed.

As soon as they finished, Anachelle got up to take his plate. Ture appeared out of nowhere to tsk at her. Removing them from her hands, he carried them to the sink.

Sighing, she gave Maris a droll stare. "I feel like an invalid."

"I think he's taking revenge on you for the way I treated him while he was wounded."

She sat down. "Really?"

"Yes, it's true. I wouldn't let him lift anything. I was quite demanding."

"He was quite annoying in a very sweet and precious way." Ture poured him a glass of dessert wine.

Maris frowned at him. "Are you trying to get me drunk?"

"Depends. . .would it work?"

Maris smiled. "Sorry. I know my limits and I never go near them."

"Too bad. But this won't. It's barely alcoholic and it enhances the aftertaste of the chocolate. Try it."

Anachelle reached for another napkin. "You might as well. He's always right about food. . .People, not so much." She took her juice from Ture's hand. "Thank you, boss."

"You're welcome." He ran back to put out a fire.

Literally.

Maris started to get up, but Anachelle stopped him.

"Don't worry. Happens a lot with the newer chefs. Ture only freaks when it catches someone else on fire."

"Someone?"

"Cooking can be deadly."

After a few minutes, Ture came back to the table. "Was I right about the wine, or was I right?"

"Yes, you were. About everything. I honestly have to say that was the best meal I've ever eaten. Thank you so much for it."

Ture beamed.

Anachelle grimaced and let out an audible groan. "Ah no, you've fed the beast. Mari? How could you betray me so? I have to live with that massive ego that already takes up half the apartment!"

Ture rolled his eyes. "You need to go on home and get some sleep for me."

"I still have another hour on the clock."

"Don't worry about it. Head on before traffic picks up."

She grinned at Maris. "Dang, I should have gotten knocked up by a bastard jerk a long time ago." Rising, she paused by Ture's side and kissed his cheek. "I'll see you later."

Ture slung the towel in his hand over his shoulder then turned back to Maris.

"How long have you been friends?" Maris asked.

"A good five years. She's an angel, but the baby's father is the son of a senator. I don't know which one. That bastard has made her life hell. He had her thrown out of her old apartment and has been causing all kinds of trouble for her."

"Why?"

"He wants her to leave the planet and vanish. My fear is he might have her killed."

Maris saw red at that. "You want to move her to the palace for protection?"

Ture cringed. "I would hate to impose."

"I can speak for Darling. The place is large enough no one would even know she was there. And he would extend the invitation himself if he were here, especially given it's one of the CDS family members who's harassing her."

Ture loved how protective both Maris and Darling were of those around them, even strangers. "I can ask her, but we commoners are a little intimidated by the places you frequent so naturally."

Maris smirked. “I don’t know what you’re talking about. I see *nothing* common about you, or Anachelle.”

Ture smiled at the unexpected compliment. That was why he loved Maris so much. No matter what he said or did, the man made him feel special and comfortable.

Safe and protected.

Wanted.

Things he hadn’t felt since he was seventeen and his father had caught him kissing his first boyfriend and thrown him out of the house.

You’re disgusting! Damn you to hell! I can’t believe I buried my daughter and not you! Get out. I hope you die of an infection before any of my friends find out about you!

To this day, neither of his parents would speak to him. And the cold brutality of their actions was nothing compared to the words they’d said that were still branded into his soul.

The worst part? His parents had called his boyfriend’s mother and father to tell them, and in retaliation, his boyfriend had beaten the hell out of him for it. Ture still bore the scar on his left cheek from his boyfriend’s class ring that had torn into his face as Devilyn rained punches down on Ture’s face.

But that was a long time ago and he refused to think of it anymore.

Maris stood up and looked about awkwardly. “How much do I owe you for the food?”

“No charge, love. My gift of thanks to you. For everything.”

“Thank you, then.” Maris hesitated. “I guess I should leave you to your work.”

“I’d rather you stay.”

Maris swallowed hard at words that meant a lot more to him than they should. *You need to go.*

But he didn’t really want to. “Are you sure?”

He nodded. “We’re only open for another thirty minutes, anyway.”

"Then I shall wait here."

Ture adored the way Maris phrased things. He was so proper and yet flamboyant and fun to be around. Some of it stemmed from the fact that he still wasn't completely fluent in Universal, and some of it was that he liked to keep others off-kilter where he was concerned. "Actually, you'd probably be more comfortable in my office while we close down. I tried to get Ana to use it, but she has a weird aversion. She's afraid the rest of the staff will hate her for her special treatment." Ture led him to the backroom that was furnished with a small desk covered in papers and a wall monitor and comfortable leather sofa. "You don't have to stay here, but it is where I spend a great deal of my time."

Maris gave a curt bow. "Then I shall be here when you finish."

Ture turned away then spun about so fast that Maris barely realized he'd done it. Before he could react, Ture pulled him into his arms and kissed him with a passion that made his head reel.

Maris growled deep in his throat as he wrapped his arms around Ture's lean, ripped body and held him close. He hungered for Zarya's friend a lot more than he should. A lot more than made any kind of sense to him.

Ture slid his hand down Maris's back and pressed his hips against his until he felt the fact that Ture was as hard for him as he was for Ture.

Damn it.

Why couldn't his body, for once, listen to his brain?

"This is a mistake," he breathed against Ture's lips. He knew it with every part of himself.

Fisting his hand in Maris's hair, Ture teased his earlobe with his tongue, sending even more chills over his body. "I swear to you, Mari. . .I won't *ever* be your mistake. Let me give you the love you deserve."

Those words carved themselves into his heart and burned with an indescribable pain.

Wanting to believe Ture in spite of a past that had taught him better, Maris met his gaze and saw the sincerity that emblazoned there. Could he trust it? "Ture. . .I can't be hurt anymore. I'm tired of it." Clenching his teeth, he winced at the bad memories that scarred him soul deep. "See, here's what's going to happen should we tangle our lives. You're going to tell me that it doesn't bother you that I'm in love with a straight man, thinking you can drive Darling out of my heart and life. For a few days, weeks or months, we'll have fun. But after awhile you'll start to get annoyed when Darling calls and I take it, no matter what's going on or how naked we are. Then one day or night, I'm going to call *you* darling and you won't know if it's an endearment or if I'm pretending you're him. Then you'll start hating me and this will end badly. It always does."

Ture scowled at him. "Good grief, Mari, what kind of insecure assholes have you dated?"

He laughed bitterly. "They're not insecure *until* they date me."

Ture pressed his forehead against Maris's in a way similar to how Maris held Darling at times. "Yes, they were. Because I can swear to you that I will *never* be jealous of your love for Darling. It's the loyalty and love you have for him that I treasure. It shows the true depth of your character and heart that you can be there for him without question or hesitation when there's nothing more to be gained from it than platonic friendship." He kissed Maris's forehead. "I don't want to drive Darling out of your heart or replace him in any way. I just want to share you sometimes. Believe me, I understand split and heavy obligations."

Still, Maris was unsure. "You say that now, but—"

"I will say it tomorrow, too." He took Maris's hand into his and led it to his groin so that he could press it against his hard cock. His gray eyes burned Maris deeply with their love and sincerity. "Just think about it, Mari. Trust me. If you're still here when I close then I can promise you a night you won't soon forget. And if you leave. . .I'll be heartbroken. But I'll understand and we can go on as nothing more than civil, platonic friends."

Yeah, but like Ture, he wanted more. He craved the same fairytale that Darling shared with Zarya. To have that one person in his life he could count on. To go to sleep and wake up in the arms of someone who would grow old with him. Someone he could trust not to hurt or judge him for things he couldn't help.

Someone who accepted him, faults and all.

Maybe his family had been right. Maybe he didn't deserve anything.

Still, he hoped.

And he hated himself for it.

Praying he wasn't about to make another awful mistake, Maris nodded.

Ture pressed his face against Maris's hair so that he could inhale his scent. "I won't hurt you, Mari. My heart is scarred and in pieces, too. I don't trust lightly, but I want to trust you."

Those words brought tears to his eyes. He cupped Ture's face in his palm. "I will be here. Waiting."

"Then I will close quickly. . .before you change your mind." He gave him a light kiss then pulled away.

TERRIFIED MARIS WOULD GROW BORED and leave, Ture rushed to close and get everything cleaned and cleared so that his people could go home and he could be with Maris. But for some stupid reason, it took twice as long to do the simplest task.

Please don't leave, Mari. . .

Damn you, fate, for conspiring against me.

By the time he returned to his office to do the last bit of paperwork, he had a sick feeling in the pit of his stomach that he was too late.

It evaporated the minute he opened the door and found

Maris sleeping on his couch. A slow smile spread across Ture's face as he noted how very boyish and sweet Mari appeared. His long legs were bent, and yet they still dangled over the edge of it. He'd taken his jacket off and used it as a makeshift blanket while he had his head resting on his arm. Never had he seen Maris more at ease.

Or more delectable.

The need to rake his hand over that luscious sight was so compelling that he wasn't sure how he resisted. But he didn't want to disturb him until he could give Maris his full attention. Silently, he started for his desk. But the instant he moved, Maris shot off the couch into a lethal pose.

He relaxed as soon as his gaze focused on Ture. "Sorry. I should have warned you that I'm a light sleeper."

No kidding. One who came awake like a soldier, ready to battle.

Ture filed that away as a warning not to make any sudden move while Maris slept. "No problem. I have a little bit of paperwork to finish in here, and I didn't want to disturb you."

Maris picked his jacket up from the floor. "Do you need me to leave?"

"No." Ture blushed as he realized how fast and forceful that response came out. "I mean—"

Maris cut his words off with a laugh. "Why are we so nervous around each other? I haven't danced around a man like this since the days before I told Darling I was gay, and I was terrified he'd find out and hate me."

Because I've never been in love with a man like this before. . .

Ture barely caught those words. They were the truth. He had a hunger for Maris unlike anything he'd ever known. But it was too soon to tell him that. "I don't know. I think it's your fierce aura that intimidates me."

"My fierce aura?"

Ture nodded. "It's like being in the same room with an exotic wild beast. You're sleek and beautiful. Every movement is a symphony of grace. And at the same time, I know how easily you can take a life and not blink. How fast you can erupt into a bloodthirsty assassin."

"I'm not bloodthirsty."

Ture closed the distance between them to straighten the folds in Maris's shirt. "But I've seen you kill without remorse. And I've had a bad run of people who've hurt me. So. . .yes, you make me a little nervous. I don't want you to have some bad flashback and kill me."

He cupped Ture's face in his palm as those dark eyes scorched him with their intensity. "I would never hurt you, Ture." Maris lowered his lips to his and gave him thc gentlest kiss he'd ever known.

Ture closed his eyes and savored being held again. How he hoped this wasn't the mistake Maris feared it to be. "I think my paperwork can wait."

Maris pulled back with a deep, sweet laugh. "Work first. I'll still be here and I'll still be hard for you."

His eyebrow shot north at the last bit. It was so out of character for his prim and proper soldier-statesman.

Maris kissed his brow and stepped back then gently nudged Ture toward his desk. "Quicker you get done. . ."

Quicker he could dine on what he hungered for most.

Biting his lip, Ture went to run the receipts and batch the credit slips while placing reorders for the morning. All the while, his gaze kept wandering over to Maris, who sat on the couch with his link in his hands. "What are you doing?"

An adorable smile curled his lips. "I'm a fierce gamer. Right now, I'm slaughtering Hauk who's playing against me."

That surprised him. He would have never guessed Maris was one of *those*. "You game?"

Maris shrugged. "It was part of our training when I was a soldier and while I don't relish a real kill, fake body counts entertain me to no end."

"I would never have thought that of you."

"I know, right? Underneath all this mountain of incredible sexiness beats the heart of a little kid."

Ture laughed at the image in his head. A part of him envied Darling for the long past he'd had with Maris. "What were you like as a child?"

"Brooding. Aggravating. Temperamental. . .Haven't really changed, now that I think about it."

"I wouldn't classify you as brooding or temperamental."

Maris flashed a grin. "No disclaimer on aggravating. Noted."

Ture laughed again. "You are not aggravating, Mari."

"Just wait. You haven't seen me in the morning. I assure you, I have PMS until two. . .sometimes three in the afternoon. Not even Darling wants to deal with that bitch."

"I've heard sex cures those symptoms."

Maris looked up from his game. "Excuse me?"

Ture shrugged playfully. "It's what the women who work for me say. Not that I know. I've never slept with a woman. Have you?" He knew from what Maris had told him a few weeks back that, unlike him, Mari had at least made an attempt. But he didn't know if Maris had ever gone through with it.

A nice shade of red crawled up from his neck to cover his face. "I was engaged to a woman once."

That disclosure floored him. Funny how that had never once come up. "Really?"

Maris nodded as he returned to his game. "I love her still, but not like that. She's more of a little sister. Which is why I couldn't go through with the wedding and how I knew beyond a doubt that I was gay. She wanted children and I didn't want to force her, and them, to live a lie with me. And to answer your earlier question, I had more than my fair share of women. Believe me, I tried everything I could to be straight. I really did. The last thing I ever wanted was to tell my family of blue-blooded ruthless military heroes and assassins that their son wasn't like everyone else. I knew none of them would take it well, and they did not disappoint my fears."

"It must have been hard for you."

Maris sighed. "I don't think it's easy on anyone. No one wants to be different, especially not when they're young."

That was true. Like Maris, he'd done his best to deny it, too. But in the end, it'd been a futile battle. No matter what he did, he kept coming back to the undeniable fact that his body just didn't react to a woman the way it did to a man.

Neither did his heart.

"So how did you break it to Darling?"

Maris laughed. "I didn't. He caught me drooling."

Cringing, Ture couldn't imagine how frightening that had to be. "Did he hurt you?"

"No, he couldn't have cared less. That's what I love about him. He told me that it made no never mind to him that I was gay, but that if I ever grabbed *his* junk, I'd be missing mine."

Ture arched a brow.

"It was funnier when Darling said it. Usually I'm funnier, too. But I'm back to that nervousness you evoke."

Ture left his desk and moved to stand in front of Maris. "I find it hysterical that I make *you* nervous when you're the one who's been trained to kill."

He turned the game off and rose to his feet. The heat in his gaze seared Ture. "I shouldn't be here. I shouldn't even be contemplating this."

"I told you, Mari. I'm a grown-up. I don't play those childish games with people's emotions. I respect what you share with Darling and I always will. All I want is a chance to prove to you that not everyone is an asshole. That I can share you and treat you the way you deserve to be treated."

He cupped Ture's cheek in his hand. "Don't break my heart, Ture. It's been shattered enough."

Ture pulled him into his arms so that he could show him just how much he wanted to be a part of his world. Closing his eyes, he breathed Maris in. "Come home with me, Mari. Let me hold you like I've been dying to since the moment I saw you skidding into my cell with both blasters blazing."

He laughed at that. "All right. Take me home and I'm yours."

Without another word, Ture locked up the restaurant and led him to his transport.

Maris was even more nervous than he'd been as he watched the shadows and light play against Ture's perfect features. While his body was still healing from the damage the League had done to him, Ture had very few external injuries left. Maris hoped none of his own healing injuries interfered with his plans tonight. All he wanted was to make love to Ture until they were both unable to walk.

"What do you do in the rain?" Ture asked out of the blue.

"Excuse me?"

"Weird random thought about when you were in the pool. You said that torrential downpours could expose you. What do you do on rainy days?"

"Try to stay in. If we have to go out, we wear a lot of rain gear and make sure the rain doesn't touch our skin."

"Have you ever been accidentally exposed?"

"Not as an adult. The last time it happened, an asshole at school had thrown me outside the locked doors of our gym in a record storm while I was changing clothes. Darling came out to find me and helped me to hide it until I went back to normal."

"I can see why you love him."

"Yeah. . .He's seen me through a lot of hell."

Ture turned a corner. "I'm amazed, given your uniqueness, that your parents sent you to a school with humans. Is that normal?"

"Not at all. Most Phrixians never even meet a human. The few who do usually only meet them in battle. I was the unfortunate exception."

"Why?"

"League mandate. They wanted a member of the

immediate ruling family to study human behavior so that we wouldn't be so warring against them. They couldn't take Kyr because he was heir at that time, so my father held a random drawing for the rest of us, and mine was the name the computer spat out."

Ture heard the bitterness in Maris's tone. "You really don't like humans, do you?"

"I didn't like my classmates. Humans are all right so long as they're human."

He couldn't agree more. "Did the League's plan work?"

"Might have had the gay son not been sent. As it was, my father blamed my personal choice on the exposure to an inferior species at such an impressionable age. In the end, all it did was fuel Kyr to rise up in the League ranks and wage his own war against the rest of the worlds. And my father now hates all humans with an unreasoning madness."

"I'm sorry, Mari."

"Thanks, but you didn't do it. I don't know what happened to Kyr. He wasn't soulless until he was seventeen. Something he won't talk about changed him forever. Whatever it was, it killed what little compassion he had and turned him into the monster he is today."

Ture heard the sadness and regret in Maris's tone. "You still love him?"

"He's my brother. I'm not the one who disowned him. And even though I don't agree with his actions or opinions, it doesn't sever the blood tie we share."

That was the heart that had won Ture's affections.

Ture pulled up to a small parking garage and docked. Maris got out first and waited until Ture joined him. It was a nice apartment building just a few blocks from the restaurant. A uniformed doorman let them in.

Maris didn't speak as they entered the lift that took them to the top floor. Ture's place was at the end of a long, elegant hall.

Ture unlocked the door. "I'm hoping Anachelle's asleep."

"She's not asleep," Anachelle called from a bedroom in back. "But she's closing her door and putting on her noise-cancelling headphones. You two have all the fun you want and don't even think about me being here. My room fridge is fully stocked and I'm locked up for the night."

Maris laughed. "I really like her."

"So do I. Let me check on her and I'll be right back."

Maris stayed in the living room, but he could hear their playful exchange as Ture fussed at her for being awake and not resting.

"Go mother the boyfriend you don't have and tell him that yes, my feet are up. I'm fine, Grandma."

Ture was still smiling as he returned, shaking his head. "She's incorrigible." He headed for the kitchen. "Would you like some wine?"

"I better not. I don't want to be tipsy."

Ture arched a brow at that.

"I had a bad drug and drinking problem for a while. Really don't want to go back to it."

"Sorry. I didn't know."

Maris draped his jacket over the back of a chair. "It's not something people wear on a scanable collar around their necks. Hey, Universe, I'm a recovering addict."

"If it makes you feel better, I had a brief bad period myself."

Maris locked a gaze with his that sent a shiver down his spine. "Doesn't make me feel better for you. It sucks to be all alone in hell."

"But you always had Darling."

Maris didn't comment. There had been a brief time, due to his own stupidity, when he'd been alone. But he tried not to think about that.

And he prayed to the gods that he never had to go through something like that again.

Ture came up behind him and wrapped his arms around Maris's waist. "I have to say you look delectable tonight, but nothing like what I expected."

He sucked his breath in as Ture teased his earlobe with his teeth. "I'm not always a flamboyant queen. I do have occasional moments of screaming normality."

"It makes no never mind to me how you dress, Mari. I adore all facets of your personality." He slid his hand down to cup him while he continued to swirl his tongue around Maris's ear. His breathing turned ragged.

Leaning back, Maris ran his hand through Ture's hair, and closed his eyes while he savored the sensation of being held and touched again. It'd been way too long. And it made him ache for the one thing that had always eluded him.

A real relationship with someone who could give as much as he took.

He was so tired of selfish users. Of people who were even more emotionally damaged than he was.

His heart pounding, he captured Ture's lips as Ture sank his hand down into Maris's pants to stroke him. He growled at how good it felt.

"You are really hard."

Maris smiled. "I've been like this since you called."

Ture's eyebrow shot north.

Turning to face him, Maris wrinkled his nose. "I have stamina the likes of which is legendary." He pulled Ture's shirt off then brushed his hand over his muscular chest. "And while you may be master of the kitchen, your skills pale in comparison to what I can do in a bedroom."

"By all means, let me see these skills of which you speak, my lord." Ture gasped as Maris picked him up and carried him as if he weighed nothing. While Ture wasn't weak by any means, Maris's strength was inhuman.

Literally.

Ture guided him to the bedroom. When he started to turn on the lamp, Maris stopped him.

"I work better in the dark."

Knowing how self-conscious Maris was about his physical scars, Ture pulled his hand back. "Next time, I want light and I think I'm highly offended that you just called this work."

Deep laughter rang rumbled in his ear as Maris laid him on the bed. "Fine then, I pleasure better in the dark."

"That still doesn't sound right."

"Yes, well, I can use my tongue for speaking to you, or for. . ."

Ture gasped as Maris teased his nipple. Chills spread the length of his body as he hardened to the point of pain. "By all means, don't let me interfere with *that*."

Another warm laugh thrilled him as Maris made a slow, deliberate and hot trail from his nipple to his abdomen. He expelled a deep breath as Maris tongued his navel while he masterfully undid Ture's pants. Lifting his hips, he allowed Maris to slide them off along with his shoes and socks.

Then, Maris suckled his toes. His eyes rolled back in his head as pleasure assaulted him. He'd had no idea how good *that* could feel. Maris ran his fingers and tongue around and between each digit then to the arch of his foot.

No wonder Anachelle had looked so pleased while Maris massaged her feet. It was incredible.

Maris nipped Ture's heel with his teeth then slowly worked his way up Ture's muscular legs. The scent of his skin filled his head, making him drunker than any wine. Since the moment Maris had first seen him, he'd been dying for this. Any man who could have humor while under fire. . .

Not to mention, the loyalty he'd given Zarya.

His heart pounding, Maris brushed his hand against Ture's cock and delighted in the pleasure he saw on Ture's face. Unlike a human, Phrixians could see as well in total darkness as they could in broad daylight—a courtesy of being amphibious. Since light couldn't penetrate to the depths of the water where many of them lived, they'd developed that ability long ago.

He nipped at Ture's hipbone while Ture buried his

hand in his hair and massaged his scalp. It felt so good to be touched again. So good to be with someone he could respect.

Starving for the intimacy, he brushed his lips over Ture's tip then drew him slowly into his mouth.

Ture cried out as Maris swallowed him whole. He shook all over at the sensation of Maris's breath and tongue on his body. Never had anyone been so thorough with him. Maris hadn't been exaggerating his skills in the least. It was as if Maris took his pleasure from giving it to others.

Careful and slow so as not to hurt him, Ture thrust his hips against Maris's head while Maris's hands skimmed his body, heightening every lick.

Ture wanted to stay like this, to savor it for as long as he could, but true to Maris's boasting. . .He couldn't last. Maris wrung too much pleasure from Ture's body. All too soon, he came in an explosion of pure ecstasy.

And still Maris tasted him. He didn't flinch or pull back. Not until he'd sucked every last bit of pleasure from him.

Panting and weak, Ture lay there with his head spinning. "That was amazing."

Maris didn't speak as he slowly kissed his way up Ture's stomach until he reached his nipple again. He seemed to have a fondness for that. His tongue swirled around it while Maris lifted Ture's hips. He pulled back slightly then slid himself inside.

Ture groaned out loud as Maris thrust against him with unbelievable skill. "Harder, Mari."

Maris bit his lip as he savored those words. Cupping Ture's cheek, he stared into his eyes. "You're beautiful."

Ture turned his face so that he could kiss Maris's palm. "I pale in comparison to you."

There he was wrong. Maris was scarred inside and out. Too many years of trying to live a lie, of trying to please people who hadn't cared about him, had taken its toll. He'd been through hell and had been seared by every flame.

But right now, with Ture, he almost felt normal. It

made no sense to him. Yet for some reason, it was like being home.

He stared into those intelligent gray eyes and lost himself completely. An instant later, he shook as his own release finally came.

Ture held him close while he played in Maris's hair. A sweet smiled curved his lips. "When did you take your clothes off?"

Maris laughed over the fact that Ture hadn't even noticed as he'd slowly stripped in between pleasuring him. "Told you, I'm *that* good."

"Yes, baby, you are."

Maris moved to Ture's side so that he could pull him into his arms and hold him.

Ture placed his hand over Maris's as he leaned against his chest and threw one leg over Maris's thighs. "I shudder at how many people you've been with to acquire your level of expertise."

Cringing at something he hated to think or talk about, Maris sighed. Unfortunately, he also knew better than to lie about it. Sooner or later, Ture would find out and either he could accept it or he'd walk. And if he was going to walk, Maris would rather Ture leave now before any more of his affections took root. "You want the truth?"

"No. . .but yes. I don't like lies."

With a deep breath for courage, Maris braced himself for Ture's anger and moral condemnation. "I was a whore."

"Mari, you shouldn't insult yourself like—"

"No, Ture. I was a trained prostitute. Bought and sold."

Ture stiffened. "What?"

Here it comes. . .

"Don't worry. I'm not diseased. I've been thoroughly tested." He ground his teeth as pain surged forward to slice open his heart. "And it was a lifetime ago. . .When my parents found out I was gay, they disowned me. My father took everything I had and destroyed it. Even my clothes, and the money I'd legally earned and saved. All my assets were seized by the Phrixian government—beauty of having noble parents with political pull. I had nothing except the battlesuit on my back, and the handful of credits in my pocket. I was too embarrassed to tell Darling. . .or anyone, for that matter, how they'd done me. Humiliated and wanting to get away from the horrors of my life, I ran. Since I didn't want to sign on as a soldier or assassin, and I had absolutely no other marketable skills, I ended up with the first guy willing to take me in. I thought he cared about me, but he was a slaver, looking for easy marks. Within a week, he'd hooked me on drugs and sold me to a brothel."

"Oh sweetie. . ."

Maris savored the lack of condemnation as Ture brushed his hand through his hair and kissed him lightly on the lips.

"I'm so sorry, Mari. How long were you there?"

"Longer than I want to admit to. I'd probably still be there had Darling not busted hell itself open to find me, risking his own safety with his uncle to do so. By the time he located me, I was so high and sick I didn't even recognize him."

But Maris would never forget the sight of Darling as he wrapped a blanket around Maris to cover his naked body on that soiled, disgusting bed in the room where he'd been imprisoned and chained. Furious over what had been done to Maris against his will, Darling had held him close to his chest. He'd been equally as furious that Maris had failed to go to him when he needed help.

"Darling held me to his heart and told me that he was taking me home with him, slaver be damned. That he would never let me suffer so long as he lived. And he had to fight hard to get me free. Trained whores are worth a lot of money. They sent everything they had to stop him." And Darling had cut through them and carried Maris out.

He smiled down at Ture. "As a token of my eternal gratitude for rescuing me, I threw up all over him on the way home. He didn't say a single word about it. Instead, he took me to his friend Nykyrian and they, with Syn, nursed me back to health. And as soon as I was safe, Darling found the guy who'd sold me and the slaver who'd owned the brothel and tore them apart."

"For that alone, I love Darling."

Maris scoffed. "You say that now. . ."

Ture rose up to stare down at him. "I will always say it, Mari. He saved you for me. I owe him for that."

Still, Maris didn't believe it. He'd had too many guys tell him that they would never be jealous of Darling and in time, none of them had been able to tolerate the fact that if Darling called for him, he'd go without hesitation.

Day or night.

He owed Darling too much not to.

Maris pulled Ture against him and cradled his head against the center of his chest. He shifted slightly so that Ture's body lay between his legs. "What about you? How did your parents react when they found out?"

"As well as yours. My dad slung everything I owned onto the lawn and set fire to it. Then they moved and made sure I didn't have their new address. They were mortified at the thought of anyone learning the truth, so they told all our friends and family that I'd died. They even held a funeral."

Maris flinched as raw anger went through him. He'd never understand the cruelty of others. Especially not against their own children. "You're kidding?"

Ture shook his head.

Maris sighed in sympathetic pain. "My mother burned my birth registration and my father had all my records deleted from the Phrixian government files. There for a time, I couldn't get anything. . .couldn't even rent a place to live. Poor Syn had to forge me all new records. But it's okay. He shaved two years off my age for me."

Ture laughed. "Are you serious?"

Smiling, he nodded. "I have great friends."

"And I have an incredible lover." Ture scooted up to kiss him.

Maris closed his eyes and cherished those words and the sensation of Ture's body on top of his. This was why he'd flitted from one lover to the next more often than most people changed their bedsheets. *Keep relationships physical and short, with no real commitment or feelings.* It was a lot easier than having his heart broken. But to be honest, he'd kill for the comfort of knowing the person with him wouldn't let him go. That he was their world and would remain so, forever.

Just once.

Rolling to his side then scooting back in bed, Ture spooned against him. Maris smiled as he buried his face against the nape of Ture's neck and inhaled the warm scent of his skin. Honestly, he'd missed Ture more than he wanted to admit. Since Ture had returned home, Maris had felt strangely adrift. Like something was missing.

But that feeling was completely gone now. He felt better than he had in a long time.

Ture's head rested against his biceps and Maris's other arm was draped over Ture's ribs so that he could hold him close to his chest. Closing his eyes, he lost himself to this one perfect moment and tried not to think about the day that would come when Ture learned to hate him and storm out of his life.

But nothing ever lasted. Not the bad. . .

And especially not the good.

Chapter 6

Maris came awake to an empty bed, but the most incredible scent he'd ever smelled wafted through the room. It made his stomach rumble and cramp in hunger. Salivating, he left the bed and saw the robe that Ture had left draped over his clothes in a nearby chair.

He pulled it on then went to investigate the warm aroma. Cautious, he kept his eyes pealed for Anachelle who was either still barricaded in her room, or gone. Since he had as many scars on his legs as he did the rest of his body, he didn't like for others to see him. Had the hunger pangs not been so ferocious, he'd have dressed first.

Following his nose, he found Ture alone in the kitchen.

As if he sensed his presence, Ture turned with a smile. "Hey, sweetie. Did you sleep well?"

Amazingly, he had. "I did. You?"

"Like a baby." Ture placed a quick kiss on his lips then returned to his cooking.

"Where's Anachelle?"

"She left a few minutes ago for a doctor's appointment." He handed Maris a glass of juice. "Freshly squeezed, it's my own juice and spice blend that's guaranteed to wake up even the most diehard night owl."

Good luck with that. Not even military drills had managed that, hence about half his physical scars. But as Maris drank it, it did wake him, and it was delicious. "Damn, you *are* a god in the kitchen."

"I prefer goddess." Ture wagged his eyebrows proudly.

Smiling, he stepped closer. "Can I do anything to help?"

"Want to chop the onion?" Ture gestured toward the island where one waited.

Maris moved to the cutting board. Next to it, Ture had cubed a steak. He took the knife that was between the two items then reached for the onion.

Ture let out a squeal of protest. "Oh my God, stop! Don't move."

Baffled by the panic in Ture's tone, he frowned. "What?"

"I swear, you're as deadly in the kitchen as you are in battle."

Completely confused, Maris stared at him. "What?" he repeated.

Ture took the knife from his hand. "Cross contamination. Didn't your mother teach you anything?"

"Not about cooking. Princes aren't exactly allowed to do that. For that matter, I don't even know which part of our palace held the kitchen."

Ture paused. "I forgot for a minute that you were royalty. Anyway, you never use the same cutting board or knife on protein that you use on your vegetables. Gracious, man. You'll kill us all!"

Maris laughed at his indignation. "Sorry."

Ture squeezed his arm as he nudged Maris away from the uncooked food. "Can you scramble an egg?"

"I can try. Never done it before, but I am good at scrambling people's thoughts. How much harder is it to confuse a nonverbal egg?"

Ture shook his head. "Come here, and let me show you how it's done."

Maris obeyed. Ture pulled him to stand between him and the stove where a pan holding some oil was heating over an open flame. Taking his hand in his, Ture led it to the eggs and pulled one out. He showed Maris how to crack it with one hand and put it in the pan then use a spatula to scramble it.

It was actually kind of neat.

Next, Ture showed him how to put the egg on a plate then he drizzled a reddish sauce over it. "Look, you now know how to cook."

Maris smiled proudly. "I can feed myself. Who knew?"

Suddenly, Ture grimaced. "Well, yes, you can cook an egg now, and die in the process."

"How so?"

Ture picked Maris's hand up and turned it to show the raw egg white on his skin. "Germs, baby. They're a more silent killer than the League's finest assassins." He pulled Maris over to the sink so that he could wash it off.

To his surprise, Ture didn't move away. Rather he washed Maris's hands for him and toyed with the webbing that elongated from the prolonged water contact.

Maris held his breath at the sensation of Ture's fingers sliding in between his and over his skin and webbing that was always much more sensitive in his aquatic form. It raised chills all over him. And he noticed the change in Ture's breathing, too.

He turned the water off then slid his hand down Maris's chest, opening his robe so that he could skim his hand over Maris's skin. Sucking his breath in sharply, Maris leaned back in Ture's arms and cupped his head in his hand. He could feel how hard Ture was against his buttocks. "Remind me to always leave egg on my hand when I'm in your kitchen."

Ture laughed in his ear as he sank his hand down to gently stroke him while he pulled the robe from Maris's shoulders and dropped it to the floor. Reaching around to his back, Maris tugged Ture's pants down until he could return the favor. Ture tongued his ear, making him even hotter before Ture accepted the invitation and slid himself inside.

Maris growled in pleasure while Ture thrust against him and stroked his cock.

Ture's hot breath fell against his neck as he nibbled and toyed with his skin. Maris sucked his breath in sharply. "I love how you feel."

"You, too, baby." Ture laved his neck as he stroked him even faster.

"Oh shit. I thought you'd be alone."

They both froze at the sound of a masculine voice in the doorway. Tall, blond, and extremely handsome, the man appeared to be in his mid-twenties.

Ture stepped back immediately and jerked his pants up, then moved around to block the man's view of Maris who quickly grabbed the robe from the floor and put it on while he tried to calm his breathing.

"What the hell are you doing here, Bristol? You were supposed to meet me at the restaurant. Later."

"I couldn't wait to see you." His blue eyes went to Maris. They narrowed dangerously with a hatred that struck Maris like a physical blow. "I had no idea I'd be interrupting you with another man."

Ture growled low in his throat. "I'll be right back." He grabbed Bristol by the arm and hauled him out of the room.

Maris could hear them arguing in a low tone, which made him all the more curious about Bristol. Who was he?

Most importantly, what was he to Ture?

Had Ture lied to him about having another lover?

As Maris headed to the bedroom to shower, Bristol came out of Ture's office and arched a brow at him. He raked a penetrating grimace over Maris's body. "You look really familiar. Do you work at Ture's restaurant?"

"No."

"Bristol!" Ture barked. "Leave him alone and go. Now!"

"Yes, Your Royal Highness." Bristol turned back to Maris. "I hope he treats you better than he's treated me." With those parting vicious words, he left.

Ture came out of the office and froze as he caught

the expression on Maris's face. He looked like he'd been kicked in the groin. But worse than his ghostly pallor was the hurt in his dark eyes.

Damn you, Bristol, you asshole!

When he reached to touch Maris, Maris stepped back.

"Mari, he's my brother," he said quickly. "I swear. He only comes around when he wants money from me."

Maris expelled an elongated breath as those words finally took the sting out of his hurt emotions. "Really?"

Ture nodded. "I have pictures of the little punk from our childhood, as well as family photos. I'll be more than happy to show them to you. He only said that to hurt you and lash out at me. He's a rank bastard like that. Here, I'll prove it." He started back for his office.

Maris caught his arm to stop him. "You don't have to get pictures. I believe you."

Ture reversed course and pulled Maris in for a hug. "I'm so sorry. I wouldn't have you hurt for anything and I might be a lot of things, but I don't cheat on others. Ever."

Maris squeezed him tight then stepped back. "If he's such an ass, why do you keep giving him money?"

"Because I'm stupid. My sister died when we were kids and as much as Bristol annoys me, I can't stand the thought of something happening to him. Besides, he's the only member of my family who still talks to me."

Maris kissed his head. "I'm sorry, baby."

Ture placed his head on Maris's shoulder. "Loyalty sucks."

"Only when it's given to the wrong person."

Ture wrapped his arms around him. "You know what my fear is, Mari?"

"No, sweetie."

"That you'll discover my Darling soon, and leave me like everyone else has."

He frowned as he tried to make sense of that. "Your Darling is your brother?"

"No. My restaurant. It absolutely consumes me, and

it's why I've never kept a single boyfriend. At first, they all love the idea of getting into one of the most exclusive restaurants on the planet without a reservation, and eating for free. But after a few weeks or months, they get jealous and angry that I can't take more than a day off every couple of weeks. That it occupies my mind, night and day. That I spend almost all my waking time there. With you, men are jealous of another man. With me, it's an inanimate object that they don't comprehend."

Maris pulled back to smile at him. "I promise I will never get jealous over a building."

Ture laughed. "That's what they all say."

Maris ran his finger along Ture's jaw. "Burning passions, I get. You're a successful business owner. You can't just shut down and walk away. If the restaurant fails, you lose everything you have, and everything you've worked for. It should be your primary focus."

"You're the only one who's ever understood that."

Maris kissed him. "If that's your worst fear, put it away. I know what it takes to be successful, and I would never give you stress for taking care of business. It's like me when I was a soldier. You have to stay focused. You take your eyes off the mission and you lose your head. The last thing you need is an asshole giving you unnecessary drama for it."

"And that's why I love you, Mari."

Maris froze as those words hit him like a blow. He wanted to believe it. He did. But he couldn't. Too many people had hurt him. Love was so easy to profess. If it came too easy then it died a quick death. He knew that.

Ture cupped his cheek. "I know, Mari. I see the fear in your eyes. Like you with my restaurant, I get it. But I will prove to you that I can share you with Darling and not be jealous. I accept the fact that I will never have the part of you that he does. Rather, I want to create my own place in your heart, and I will always have the one part of you that he doesn't."

"And that is?"

Ture smiled as he cupped Maris in his hand. "This luscious body that makes me insane with lust. I swear, even if I were straight, I'd crave you."

Maris captured his lips and held him close. *Don't break my heart, Ture.* But deep inside, he knew Ture would.

Sooner or later, all men did.

Even Darling.

Chapter 7

Ture froze as he took a minute to watch Maris interacting with his staff. For the last three weeks, they'd been together night and day, almost without interruption. It still amazed him that Maris had yet to get on his nerves. He'd never been with anyone for this amount of time without having at least one argument over something.

And the staff loved Mari.

Even Bertram, and Bertram hated everyone.

His hands covered by rubber gloves, Maris stood at the sink, helping to rinse dishes since one of the dishwashers had become ill and had to leave early. Dressed in his high neck black riding suit with white reflective stripes, Maris was an odd sight with the white apron covering it. The stitched quilted leather that protected Maris's body whenever he rode his airbike hugged every inch of his muscled physique and cupped his ass in a way that should be illegal. Damn, he looked so rugged and masculine that it was hard for Ture to breathe.

Best of all, Maris had started growing his hair out for Ture. And since he hadn't shaved in two days, he had a gorgeous shadow of whiskers that didn't help Ture's hard-on in the least.

"You are so in love with him," Anachelle whispered as she paused by his side.

"That obvious?"

She nodded. "You are absolutely licking him with your eyes."

Laughing, Ture shook his head at her. "You're terrible."

"Hey, I'm not the one mentally molesting the poor man who's trying to wash dishes for you."

"Didn't anyone ever tell you it's a bad idea to harass your boss?"

"No. I must have missed that email." Wrinkling her nose playfully, she headed back to her corner to fold napkins and sort silverware.

Ture went over to the oven and pulled out his latest experiment. At least once a week, he tried something new. Luckily, it smelled good. He cut a small piece off and took it to Maris so he could be his guinea pig.

Maris pulled his gloves off before he dutifully opened his mouth and allowed Ture to place it on his tongue.

"Well?"

Maris chewed it then frowned.

Ah, crap. He'd never done that before. Ture deflated. "What's missing?"

"Something. . ." Maris bent his head down and kissed him fiercely. Pulling back, he smiled. "Yeah, that was definitely the missing ingredient." He winked. "It's perfect. Delicious. You need to try it."

Ture handed him the fork to wash and had started back for the roast when he saw a waiter who looked like he was about to cry. He diverted course toward him. "What's wrong?"

Tyryn sighed. "Obnoxious customer."

His vision darkened at those words as Tyryn reached for two plates and set them on a serving tray. "Are those for that table?"

He nodded. "Maybe the fourth time's the charm."

"Fourth?"

"It was undercooked. Over cooked. And then too cold."

Ture took the tray from his hands. "Here, I'll deal with it. You take a half hour and unwind. I'll get Glee to cover your section. . .Which table?"

"Thirty-four, and thank you, boss."

"No problem." Ture headed for the door to the dining room.

Maris frowned as he saw Ture leave with a tray and a major grimace. *That's odd.* He went over to Tyryn who was now sitting on a stool with his head in his hand as if he had a massive migraine. "Hey, what happened?"

"Two words. Ass. Holes." Tyryn sighed. "Aristos came in and decided nothing was good enough for them and that our restaurant was seriously overrated."

Maris winced. Ture would be devastated if they attacked his pride and joy. Pulling the apron off, he went to the window and peered out to see who was at the problem table. The minute his gaze focused on the troublemakers, his fury mounted. Brux Nylan and his best friend Aston Hyrun. Nylan's father was a senator who'd scandalized Darling back in the day, and had almost cost him his life. Aston was a prick both he and Darling had gone to school with. One who'd been friends with Crispin. And the same bastard who'd thrown Maris out into the rain, naked, and locked the door.

Shaking with the weight of his rage, Maris left the kitchen to back Ture who had no idea of the magnitude of viciousness he was about to encounter.

Nylan spat the food in his mouth onto the plate. "This is the worst yet. Unacceptable. How can this possibly be *the* premiere restaurant when it serves dog food?"

The look of hurt on Ture's face cut through his heart. Unable to bear it, Maris stopped next to Ture and put his hand on his shoulder. "You'll have to forgive them, Tur. They're so used to the palatableness of the boots they lick that everything else tastes strange. Perhaps if you dip their food in dirt, they'll find it more to their liking."

Aston curled his lip as he glanced about the restaurant. "Well, well, look who's here. I'm amazed Darling let you off your knees long enough to leave the palace. Or does *he* take the bitch role? I've never figured out which of you is the woman."

"Oh honey, the bitch is all me. If you had a dick at all you'd know that."

Aston shot to his feet, but Maris didn't blink or back down.

Maris raked Aston with a sneer. "You lost your tongue or your nerve?"

"I don't want to get fag blood on me and catch whatever disease you're carrying."

"Then by all means, shall I show you the door. . .or would you rather go out through a wall?"

"Come on," Nylan said, rising to his feet. "I've lost my appetite."

"You've lost more than that."

Maris looked past Nylan's shoulder to see Drake standing there with an expression on his face that said he'd heard the majority of this conversation.

Drake stepped back so that his guards would have access to the two men. "Brux Nylan and Aston Hyrun, you are both under arrest for treason and any other charge I can think of while I eat." An evil glint shone in Drake's eyes as he met Maris's gaze. "I think they're both going to find out all about the bitch position in jail."

"You can't be serious!" Aston snarled.

"This is outrageous!" Nylan shouted. "I'm calling my father."

Drake patted him on the cheek. "You do that, puddin'. I can't wait for your father to confront my brother." He smiled at Maris. "We should probably sell tickets for that event, eh, Mari?"

"Indeed."

As Drake's guards hauled them out while they screamed obscenities, Maris glanced around the shocked diners.

"Sorry for the drama everyone. Two felons being arrested is always newsworthy. But to make it up to everyone, your dinners are on me."

Ture gaped at his remarkable offer.

Drake leaned in to whisper to Maris. "I'll cover it for you."

"You don't have to."

"Then let's split it."

"If it'll make you feel better." Maris scowled. "Why are you here, anyway?"

Drake inclined his head to a beautiful blond sitting at a table. "Datc. It impressed her that I got in here—thank you for that, by the way."

Maris rolled his eyes at how little it took to make Drake happy. "Thank you for your help."

"No problem. I don't like people insulting any of my brothers." He held his hand up to Maris. When Maris took it, Drake pulled him into his arms. "Love you, bro."

"Love you, too."

Drake clapped him on the back then returned to his date.

Maris paused as he caught the strange look on Ture's face. "I'm sorry if I embarrassed you."

"You didn't embarrass me. I can't believe you came to my rescue."

Maris brushed his fingers against Ture's chin. "I told you I wouldn't let anyone hurt you. That includes insensitive guttersnipes."

Ture helped Maris clear the table as amazement filled him. No one had ever stood up for him before. He glanced over to Drake who was laughing with his companion. The prince was a lot more handsome than he appeared in state photos. And Ture could understand Maris's devotion to the royal family. They did stick together in a way few families did.

Most of all, they watched each other's backs.

When they returned to the kitchen, Maris told the

waiters to bring him the tabs for the diners who'd been present during the confrontation.

Ture touched him on the arm. "You don't have to do that."

"Yes, I do. I'm not going to have a restaurant full of people smack talk my man or his business for something I did. What kind of bitch do you think I am?"

Ture's breath caught in his throat. It was the first time Maris had referred to them as a couple or used any kind of ownership term for him. Maris hadn't even realized he'd done it as he resumed rinsing dishes.

But Ture had heard it and it brought tears to his eyes. For Maris, this was a major step.

And it meant the universe to him.

HOURS LATER, TURE WAS CLEANING out the oven when he felt Maris behind him. As he turned, Maris gave him a light, sweet kiss.

"I'm about to run the receipts for my charges. You want me to batch the rest?"

Ture was surprised by the offer. "You know how?"

Maris grinned. "I do. Ana showed me."

"Then yes. Please."

"You know, I can also enter in the orders and do payroll."

"Oh my God, I would love you forever if you did."

A wicked light entered Maris's dark eyes. "Forever?"

"And then some."

Maris squeezed his arm before he went to Ture's office to do the paperwork Ture despised with every part of his being. He'd meant what he said. If Maris hadn't been perfect before this, this would have cinched it.

"Ture?"

He looked over to Bertram.

"I finished the dining room. Is there anything else you need me to do?"

"No. I'll let you out. Thanks for helping."

"My pleasure."

It really wasn't. Bertram had bitched under his breath the whole time. But he was reliable and, most of the time, extremely efficient at his job.

Ture walked him to the front door and bid him goodnight before he locked it again and checked the bathrooms. Satisfied everyone was gone, he headed back to the kitchen to finish the last bit of cleaning and breakdown.

As soon as that was done, he went to his office to find Maris entering orders. His hands flew over the keys. He was far more proficient at it than Ture.

He started forward then stopped as he saw a large shopping bag on the couch. "What's this?" he asked with a frown.

"It was delivered right after Ana went home. It's just a few things I got for the baby."

Ture smiled. Every day something new showed up that Maris had bought for either the baby or Anachelle. "You keep this up and everyone's going to think you're the baby's father."

"I can't help it. Zarya and Darling keep emailing me for my opinion on things they're buying for their rugrat and when I see them and like them, I want them for Ana, too. Every baby needs to be spoiled."

"You're doing an awesome job of it." Ture blinked back tears at how generous Maris was. He'd never known anyone with a bigger heart, and the fact that so many had hurt him made Ture want their blood for it.

How could anyone not love and adore Maris?

He moved to stand behind the chair so that he could rub Maris's shoulders while he finished up. "How much more do you have?"

"Just this then I'm done."

"Wow, you're fast."

"This is nothing. Try doing flight reports, schematics, checks and plans every night after you've spent all day on patrol. If I forget to order shallots, no one's life is going to end and I won't burst into flames an instant before the vacuum of space rips my ship apart."

Ture cringed. "I don't like that thought."

"Neither did I. And I would have liked it a lot less had I ever done so." Leaning back in the chair, Maris looked up at him as he sent the order in. "All done."

"All done," Ture repeated as turned the chair so that Maris faced him. "Hmmm, I think that deserves a reward of some kind."

Maris arched his brow. "What kind of reward?"

Biting his lip, Ture shrugged. "I don't know. . . ."

Maris froze at the hot look in Ture's eyes as he ran his hands up Maris's thighs. He hardened instantly.

Ture straddled his legs then pulled him in for a scorching kiss.

Growling in pleasure, Maris ran his hands under Ture's shirt, over the hard muscles. "You keep this up and you'll never have to do paperwork again."

Ture laughed as he cupped Maris then undid his pants. His breathing ragged, he slid to the floor, between Maris's parted thighs. Just as he bent forward to taste him, Maris's link buzzed with the unique tone that was reserved solely for Darling so that Maris never missed his calls.

Silently, Ture cursed the man's timing.

Maris picked it up and answered it while Ture sat back on his haunches. He braced his elbow on Maris's thigh and propped his head on his hand.

"No, it's okay. Did you need something?"

Ture rolled his eyes. It really wasn't okay. At least twice a week Darling interrupted them. The only thing that kept him from cursing them both was the knowledge that Darling was the sole reason he had Maris. More than that, Darling was the reason *he* was alive right now.

So it allowed him to accept something that would have normally made him insane.

"Yeah, I'll be there in a few minutes. . .okay."

Ture sighed heavily as he closed Maris's fly.

"I'm sorry," Maris said sheepishly. "The League is stepping up their efforts on our heads and he wants to—"

Ture interrupted his words with a kiss. "It's fine, Mari. I told you. I'm not jealous. Irritated, but not jealous. And I'm not irritated at you." Darling's was the neck he wanted to wring. "Go on. I'll take Ana's gift home and have some chocolate mousse waiting for you when you get back."

Maris brushed his finger down Ture's cheek as he stared at him in wonder. True to his word, Ture had yet to get angry over Darling's calls or whenever Maris went to meet him. Instead, Ture bribed him to hurry back with evil things such as the delectable mousse he made that melted in Maris's mouth and left every tastebud in his head singing. "With extra topping?"

"Absolutely."

Maris hesitated as Ture stood back. "Are you still going to love me after you've made me too fat for my clothes?"

"There will just be more of you to love."

Rising, Maris pressed his cheek to Ture's, and closed his eyes as he savored the warm scent of Ture's skin. For the first time in his life, he was torn between wanting to stay and needing to go.

He'd almost told Darling it could wait. Never in his life had he felt that compunction.

Tonight he did.

And honestly, that scared the hell out of him. He didn't like change. He never had.

But things were changing fast and he wasn't sure if it was for the better or worse. Pulling back, he cupped Ture's cheek. "I'll return soon."

"I'll be waiting."

Maris nodded, yet as he left, he wondered how much longer Ture would be willing to wait for him on nights like this.

Chapter 8

"YOU ABOUT DONE?"

Maris looked up from the orders he was placing to catch Ture standing in the office doorway. "Almost. . .Did you really mean to order two hundred radishes?"

An evil grin spread across his gorgeous face. "I did. You have something against the mighty radish?"

Maris held his hands up in surrender. "Not the cook, but yuck. However, if anyone could possibly make something so repugnant tasty, I have all faith in your abilities."

Smiling, Ture moved to stand behind Maris's chair so that he could review the order Maris was finishing up for him. "I still can't believe you do this for me without complaint. I detest this part of the business."

Maris shrugged as he leaned back in the chair. "Paperwork doesn't bother me in the least. And it makes me feel more useful than ruining Hauk's night when I beat him online. Not to mention the real reason I do it. . ."

"And that is?"

He turned the chair around and pulled Ture into his lap. "The sooner I get you home, the sooner I can ravish you."

Biting his lip, Ture put his arms around Maris's neck. "I definitely like that thought."

Maris kissed him until someone cleared their throat. They looked at the doorway to see Anachelle standing there unabashedly.

"Guys? I really hate to intrude, but my water just broke."

With a light gasp, Ture launched himself to his feet. In a total panic, he started to Anachelle then turned back to Maris then circled around again. It would be comical if Ana didn't need to get to the hospital.

Maris caught him by the arms. "Breathe, baby. It's okay. I'll lock up and finish. . .and clean the water off the floor. You get her to the hospital, and I'll meet you there."

"Okay." He panicked even more.

"Ture," Maris said calmly. "Look at me, sweetie."

He obeyed.

"Calm down. She's not going to have the baby on you. I promise. Drive safely. It's only five blocks away. Let her out at the emergency room doors, park and then head inside. Okay?"

"Gods, I love you, Mari." He gave him a quick kiss then went to Anachelle to get her out of the restaurant.

Ana and Darling were the reasons why they always took separate vehicles to work. In case one of them had to leave, the other one had a way home.

Maris followed them to the door so that he could make sure Ture actually got her into his transport. He smiled as Ture continued to run around like a scrambled mess while he tried to help her in then went to his side of the car then came back to make sure she was inside and secured. All the while, Ture was breathing so rapidly, it was wonder he hadn't passed out.

That man did not handle a crisis well. His neurons synapsed in so many directions that he could never focus on a single thought or task. It was something his past boyfriends had despised about him, but Maris found it oddly adorable. And when it'd really mattered—when they'd been escaping the prison, Ture had managed to hold it together with a strength that still amazed him.

It was only now that he knew Ture better that he fully appreciated how hard that had been for him.

Stepping inside, Maris locked the door then cleaned up Ana's mess before he hurried through the paperwork. He had no doubt that Ture would be pacing a donut-shaped hole in the hospital floor until he got there. Maris was the only one who was able to calm him when he was in one of these frenetic moods. Mostly because he'd learned to keep a lid on his emotions in battle. And because Ture's anxiety brought out the protector in him, instead of his impatience. That one vulnerability made him feel needed.

Because other than that, Ture was extremely self-sufficient and very proud of that fact.

Maris paused as he saw a shadow at the door. Instinctively, his hand went to the small blaster he kept holstered at the base of his spine. At first Ture had been terrified of the fact that Maris was always armed, but once he saw the price on Maris's head, he'd insisted that Maris carry even more weapons than he had in the past.

And after the last round of contracts had been issued from the League against them, they were all on high alert.

Using the shadows for cover, he made his way to the front. Since the person was visible through the frosted glass, he doubted they were League trained. But it could still be a thief out to rob them.

Maris tilted his head so that he could see through the small line of clear glass while making sure that the person outside couldn't detect him. He relaxed as he recognized Bristol.

Rolling his eyes, he moved his hand away from his weapon and settled his jacket back into place. He opened the door. "Can I help you?"

"Where's my brother?"

"He's not here."

Bristol scowled as he stared at him for a minute. "You the guy I met at Ture's a few weeks ago?"

"I am."

"Wow, Ture's been with someone for over a month. That's a first." He narrowed his gaze on Maris. "Sorry, I didn't recognize you with your clothes on, and without Ture's dick in your ass. What was your name again?"

Maris profaned violence, but right now. . .He could definitely see the appeal of knocking that smugness off Bristol's face. "I didn't give it." He locked the door and set the alarm with the remote in his hand, which made Bristol even more curious.

"Ture doesn't let his boyfriends have keys to his restaurant. Where is he?"

Maris slid the security card into his pocket. "He had to leave early."

Anger snapped in Bristol's eyes as he glared at him. "Don't play this shit with me. I'm his brother. Now where is he?"

Maris ground his teeth at the frustration of dealing with this. Ture had been very insistent that he never give any information to his brother. *The less he knows, the better. . .Trust me, Mari. Don't engage him. Unlike me, he has no loyalty or inhibitions.*

Since Ture knew his brother much better than Maris did, he deferred to Ture's warning.

"I can have him call you when I see him." Maris started past, but Bristol stopped him with a rough grip that made his vision dim.

"You better answer me, you cock-sucking quim. Or I'll beat the hell out of you."

Maris dropped his voice an octave and fell into his staunch military training. "Boy, you're about to head down a path that's going to lead you to a really bad year. Now take your hand off my arm, two steps back, and you might get through the night without an ambulance ride."

Shock replaced the smirk. Still, he didn't loosen his grip. "You don't act like a faggot."

"And I don't hit like a girl, motherfucker. Now unless you're craving extensive dental work and reconstructive surgery, get out of my face."

That growl succeeded in making Bristol release him. "Who *are* you?"

"The lucky bastard who happens to be your brother's boyfriend. And I'll make sure he calls you before he sticks his dick in my ass later. Now goodnight." Maris stepped around him and went to his airbike that was parked a few feet away. As he pulled his helmet on, he glanced back to see Bristol still eye-balling him.

Whatever.

Every family had its asshole. And in Maris's case, his had a solid dozen. Putting it out of his mind, he headed for the hospital.

TURE CHECKED THE CLOCK AS his anxiety worsened. Maris should have been here already. . .

What if something happened to him?

Unable to breathe for the panic, he pulled his link out to call.

"Where's Ana?"

Relief tore through him as he heard that deep, glorious accent. Turning, he threw himself into Maris's arms. "What took you so long? You had me worried."

"Sorry. Your brother showed up while I was leaving."

"You didn't give him your name, did you?"

Maris shook his head. "You told me not to." He held the restaurant's security card out to Ture.

"Keep it."

"You sure?"

Ture nodded. "And to answer your question, Ana's doctor threw me out until I could, and I quote, get a hold of myself."

Maris gave him an adorable smile. "Sounds about right. Want to try again?"

"Sure."

Maris offered him his arm. Ture tucked his hand into his elbow and led him to Anachelle's room. She lay in the bed, chewing crushed ice while a nurse checked her vitals.

The nurse arched her brow at Ture. "Are you calm now?"

Ture rolled his eyes. "Yes, my sanity just arrived."

Her gaze practically licked Maris from head to foot. Dressed in his all black protective biker gear, he was exquisite. Especially since he'd grown his whiskers into a sexy well-trimmed beard. A slow smile spread across her face. "I hate to ask this cutie, but are you family?"

"He's the baby's father," Anachelle answered before Maris had a chance to speak.

Maris arched a brow, but didn't contradict her. After all, they'd been teasing him about acting like an expectant father for weeks now.

"Oh good," the nurse said, holding her hand out to Mari. "I'm Aundrea and I'm the nurse assigned for the delivery. I was just telling your. . ."

"Girlfriend," Anachelle supplied.

"Girlfriend that she's at three centimeters, so we should have a little time. But we shouldn't assume anything. I'm going to let the doctor know you're here, and will be right back." She left them.

Maris frowned at Anachelle. "Boyfriend?"

She shrugged. "I'd already told them that Ture was my brother so that he could stay with me while we waited for you, and I didn't want to chance them thinking you two were incestuous or something."

"Great," Maris breathed. "So instead of being your creepy incestuous brother, I'm your scuzzy boyfriend who's snaking on you *with* your brother. Lovely. Just the label I was looking for." He moved to kiss her on her cheek. "How are you feeling, sweetie?"

"It's a little painful. I won't lie. But manageable for the moment. I'm glad you two are here. In spite of what they think, you and Ture are all the family I have. Thank you both for taking care of me." Tears filled her eyes then ran down her cheeks.

Maris hugged her close. "Oh, honey. We love you. We're always here for you, you know that."

Ture held her hand. “Don’t you worry about anything, except that little boy.”

Sniffing back her tears, she nodded.

HOURS LATER, MARIS LEFT THE delivery room to find Ture asleep on a waiting room couch. Since Ana had pegged him as the baby’s father and Ture as her brother, the doctor had allowed Maris to stay and forced Ture out once serious labor began.

Shaken by it all, he knelt beside the couch and touched Ture’s arm.

Ture woke up with a jerk then frowned. “Is something wrong, baby?”

“I am *so* glad I’m not a woman.” He let out a ragged breath. “That. . .was terrifying. I’m thinking we’d better lock Darling up whenever Zarya goes into labor. It’s going to get ugly.”

Ture cupped his cheek. “How is she and the baby?”

“She’s fine and sleeping. The boy. . .It was amazing, Ture. I wish you’d been there. One minute, Ana was calling out for every set of male testicles in the universe to be cut off, and the next. . .this tiny little person was in the doctor’s hands. He gave the baby to me while they cut the cord, and I stared into these dark eyes that stared back at me. He’s so tiny and perfect. Beautiful. You want to see him?”

“Absolutely.” Ture sat up. “How are you doing?”

“Good, but exhausted.” Maris yawned then put his arm around Ture’s shoulders as he led him toward the nursery. “I’d give anything if you could carry me home.”

“Oh, baby, I wish.”

Maris stopped in front of a large window and waved at one of the attending nurses. She smiled brightly then moved to pick up one of the blue-swaddled babies. She brought him closer for Ture to see.

Tears misted in his eyes. “Oh, Mari, he *is* beautiful.”

"I know, right?"

"What did she name him?"

"Terek Andros. . .Sulle."

Ture quirked an eyebrow at that.

Grinning sheepishly, Maris shrugged. "They think I'm the father, and she had to list the father's name for his registration. At least this way his real father can't come in and use him against her later. They'll never have a record of his real name anywhere."

That was very true. "So do you have to pay child support?"

He laughed. "No. I'm going to sign away custody as soon as she can get the paperwork drawn up."

Turning back toward the baby, Ture smiled. "Hey, little Terek," he said, even though the baby couldn't hear him. Then he waved at the baby.

It was the most adorable thing Maris had ever seen. He yawned again.

Ture frowned. "I need to get you to bed."

Maris's eyes widened in acute interest as his body perked up instantly. "That's my boy."

Laughing, Ture shook his head. "Is that all you think about?"

"Of course not. Food. . .which you also give me. Damn, Tur, I think you're the perfect man."

They both froze as Maris realized what he'd said. It was the closest thing to an avowal of love that he'd made. Terror filled him.

"Relax, honey. I know you're tired and I'm not making anything big out of it." Ture walked him toward the door. "Let me get you home and tucked in."

Maris followed Ture to his transport then headed for his airbike. This was the only part of his Phrixian past that he'd really hung on to. He could still remember the stunned look on Darling's face the first time he'd seen Maris riding one.

"It's so not you."

Maris smiled as he strapped his helmet on. Darling

was right. He didn't normally go for things that messed up his hair or clothes. But he loved the freedom of it. The sensation of flying through the air at over two hundred miles an hour. . .There was nothing like that kind of freedom.

Ture hated that he drove one. He thought it was dangerous. But then so was breathing.

Maris checked his mirrors. He narrowed his eyes as he saw someone just outside the hospital, watching him. Was it attraction or nefarious?

From this distance, he couldn't tell. Still, he called it in to the Sentella so that they could set up a guard for Anachelle and the baby.

Better safe than sorry.

And as he headed back to Ture's, a new fear gripped him. Unlike Darling and the very small group of Maris's friends, Ture wasn't military trained. He was purely civ.

Defenseless.

If the League or a bounty hunter went after Ture, there was nothing he could do to protect himself.

Suddenly terrified, Maris gunned the engine and made the building in record time. He parked and locked it down fast then ran inside.

Holding his breath, he tried not to panic. But he couldn't help it.

"Ture?" He scanned the apartment.

There was no sign of him.

Even more frantic, he went through the rooms. He'd just cleared the bathroom when he heard someone out front. His heart racing, he ran down the hallway to find Ture locking the door.

Ture had barely turned around when someone seized him and shoved him back against the wall. Not painfully, but the unexpected act startled him. He started to panic until the wonderful scent of Maris's skin and cologne hit him. When he opened his mouth to ask what was wrong, Maris claimed his lips with a kiss so hot that it made his head reel. Maris held him with a desperation that was as concerning as it was incredible.

When Maris finally pulled back, he laid his head on Ture's shoulder and still kept him locked in his arms. He could feel the fierce, hard beating of Maris's heart against his chest.

"Baby? What's wrong?"

Maris drew a ragged breath. "I'm just tired. I didn't mean to scare you. Sorry."

"It's all right. I don't mind when you go all military on me. So long as you don't hurt me, I'm good with it."

He lifted his head to pierce him with a sincere stare. "I would *never* hurt you."

Extremely worried now, Ture nodded. "I know." He brushed his fingers against the beard he'd talked Maris into growing. He'd never cared for them in the past, but Maris made it look sexier than hell. "I really do love you, Mari. Insanity and all."

Maris wanted to return those words with every part of himself. But he couldn't. Especially not tonight. To say that back would dare fate to hurt Ture. To rip him out of Maris's life.

Instead, he finally stepped away so that Ture could enter his apartment. Still he couldn't shake the bad feeling in his gut. Something was wrong. Every instinct he had was on high alert.

Shrugging his jacket off, he laid it over the chair where he usually kept it.

"You know, Mari. . .I've been thinking."

His gut knotted with dread. *Here it comes. . .Get out.* He knew it was too good to last. "Yeah?"

Ture hedged, which twisted Maris's stomach into a painful knot. "I. . .um. . .would you. . ." He let out a hard breath. "Okay, I'm just going to say it. I can do this. Really. . .Would you like to move in with me? I mean, you're already here most of the time, anyway. Right?"

Maris went weak at the offer as joy ripped through him. "I'd love to."

"Really?"

"Absolutely."

Ture bit his lip as happiness filled him. He'd been wanting to ask Maris to move in, but had been too afraid to since Maris was so reluctant to say he loved him. Not that he had to. It showed in everything Maris did. Big and little. Such as taking over the paperwork so that Ture could focus on prepping the kitchen and leave a little earlier to come home. Stepping in with a willing pair of hands whenever Ture or his staff needed help. Going into the fridge for him so that he wouldn't get chilled. Letting him go first in the shower every morning so that he never had to take a lukewarm or cold bath. A million thoughtful things that came together to make Maris the sweetest, hottest lover anyone could ask for. And while Mari wasn't perfect, he tried. That more than anything meant the universe to him.

He pressed his cheek to Maris's. "Thank you."

"For what?"

"For being you, sweetie."

Maris frowned as Ture left him and headed for the bedroom. "I do love you," he whispered. But every time he tried to say it out loud, he choked on the words.

Just once in his life, he wanted everything to work out. Nothing would make him happier than to relive the last few weeks over and over again, until he died from pure joy overload. He didn't want any of it to change.

Ever.

But nothing ever lasted.

Not the bad.

And especially not the good.

Chapter 9

Maris paused as someone knocked on his bedroom door. "Come in."

Darling opened it and entered the room with a frown. "I just heard that you'd returned and. . ." His scowl deepened as he saw the bags Maris was packing. Because of his reluctance to tempt fate, Maris had spent the last two weeks moving his things over to Ture's apartment. He was hoping if he went slow enough, bad luck wouldn't take notice of him and slap him down for daring to be happy with someone else.

"You're leaving?"

Maris duplicated his scowl as he caught the hurt note in Darling's voice. "You're not jealous, are you?"

"Honestly? A little, yeah. I miss having you around, bud. I haven't seen you in weeks."

Maris tucked his shirts into his bag then closed the distance between them. He pulled Darling into his arms and gave him a light hug. "You know you're my first love."

Darling tightened his grip before he released him. "I'm not used to sharing you like this. I don't like it, Mari."

"So you do love me?" he teased.

"You know I do."

But not romantically. Darling's heart and soul would always belong to Zarya first and Maris was good with that. And now that he had Ture, he understood it better than he ever had before.

Darling swallowed hard. "Through thick and thin, brothers to the bitter end, right?"

Maris gave him a sincere stare. "Always. You need me, night or day, you know I'm here for you. Ture says he accepts that and is good with it." The gods knew, Ture had already proven it. He had yet to say anything nasty about how often Maris vanished whenever Darling beckoned.

"You really care about him, don't you?"

Maris hesitated. What he felt was so complicated. He seriously enjoyed hanging out in the restaurant with Ture and his staff. Stealing kisses in the corners when no one was looking. It didn't bother him at all that they spent sixteen to twenty hours a day there.

He even enjoyed helping Ana tend Terek in the middle of the night. Watching the baby during the day so that she could rest. It was the first time in his life that he really felt like he was home. That he was part of a family that accepted everything about him. Even his early morning crankiness.

When he'd first moved into the Caronese Winter Palace as an ambassador, Darling's uncle had made him feel like a venereal disease in a whorehouse. Arturo had gone out of his way to verbally attack him and Darling.

Then after Arturo's death, Darling had been. . .honestly, insane. For a time, he'd even feared that Darling might kill them both.

Until Zarya.

She had healed Darling and returned him to the best friend he'd been growing up. But from the moment she moved in, Darling had been preoccupied with her, leaving Maris to feel like a third wheel. They'd tried to include him, but they wanted and needed to be alone at times, and that was how it should be.

Still, he'd felt a bit abandoned and a lot lonely.

At least until Ture had come into his life. He didn't know what it was about that man, but he calmed the rage inside Maris that had simmered in his gut since the day his parents had disowned him. Ture touched a part of him that he hadn't even known he possessed. All he wanted was to be with him. And yet he lived in a state of constant fear that he would lose everything again.

It left him twisted in a knot and unsure. Terrified and anxious, and at the same time happy and serene.

None of it made sense to him.

"I'm not sure how to answer."

Darling narrowed his gaze suspiciously. "What was the first thing that entered your mind, and I know it wasn't what you just said."

Sighing, Maris stepped away. Darling knew him better than anyone. Even himself. "Yes. I like him a lot."

"Then what's the problem?"

"You know the problem." Maris looked down at his clothes and luggage. "What am I doing, Darling? I know this isn't going to last. It can't. It never does. And I'm so tired of being hurt. How did you ever forgive Zarya for betraying you?"

Darling snorted. "It wasn't easy. But this great friend of mine threw her at me and left me with no choice, except to deal with the pain of my past. And I wanted to hate her in ways you can't imagine. I craved it. Yet as hard as it was to trust her, the agony of existing without her was so much worse. There are only a handful of people in this universe I need. The thought of losing one of you sends me into a panic that is indescribable. It's why the sight of those bags on your bed pisses me off to an Andarion type of rage level. I can't protect you if you're not here."

"As long as I'm sober, I do a pretty good job of protecting my own posterior. . .and yours."

"I know. But as of last night, the League has increased

the bounty on all our heads again. At this point, your ass is worth almost twice the price of mine. I think Kyr is using you to hurt me."

"What about Zarya and Drake?"

"Zarya's a political nightmare for him that he's publicly avoiding. Who knows what he's doing in private? Likewise, he's staying away from naming my brothers and sister. He's not sure they helped rescue Zarya and Ture and the others, so legally, he can't touch them."

That made Maris feel a bit better. "Is there a price on Ture's head?"

"No. Just those of us Kyr could identify in the rescue party."

"Me, you, Nykyrian and Caillen."

He nodded. "It's just a matter of time before they start sending in their top assassins."

Maris zipped his last bag closed. "Saf will warn me before they come after me."

"If he knows. Kyr might not tell him."

Maris shook his head in denial. "Kyr doesn't know we still talk." If he did, he'd kill their little brother and then Maris would annihilate him over it. Ever since Saf had been mistaken for him and brutally attacked when his father had tried to assassinate him, Maris had been hyper protective of him.

No one touched Saf with immunity.

"It's about to get bad, Mari. I had to dispatch troops to solidify my borders an hour ago. The League is headed for our colonies and is trying to blockade and embargo us. Most of the empires have withdrawn in fear of them. They hit two of the Sentella's smaller bases yesterday, and killed almost two hundred people. They injured over a thousand more."

"I'm not afraid."

"Nor am I. Not for me. But for those I love. . .I don't want to see you hurt because I rage-hit your brother when

I should have held my temper in check."

Maris smiled at him. "I told you when we headed out to rescue Zarya that if you were going to hell, I'd be driving the bus. Bring the rain."

Darling sighed. "And it's coming, my brother. With a torrential downpour. One I don't want you caught in."

Chapter 10

Over and over, Darling's warning replayed in Maris's head as he sat in the commercial transport that was locked in traffic. He'd never been patient with such things, but today. . .

He scowled as he swept the scenery around them and a bad feeling went through him. When hunted, gridlock was a dangerous thing. It was another of the reasons he normally drove an airbike. They were virtually impossible to trap like this.

But with luggage, he'd needed a trunk. And a transport made him an easy mark.

Every ounce of his military training kicked in.

"I'll get out here," he said to the driver before he swiped his card. "Deliver my bags to the destination and I'll make sure you're well tipped."

"Yes, my lord."

Two seconds after Maris swiped his card, he cringed at the rampant stupidity. Damn, he'd lived as a civ too long. If the League was monitoring for them, he'd just given up his location. *Stupid moron.*

Cursing himself, Maris slid out of the transport and secured his smallest bag across his body so that both of his arms would be free. He didn't pause or hesitate as he maneuvered through the crowded street on foot. Making sure to keep one hand on his concealed blaster, he stayed vigilant and hated every second of it.

Even though it was ingrained in him by countless hours of training and drills, this degree of heightened alert threw him back to a time and place he didn't want to revisit.

What are you, a pathetic faggot? Keep your guard up! Only queers rely on their girlfriends to protect them. You are a soldier, not some limp-wristed pussy.

Back then, he'd lived in a state of perpetual pissed off. It'd been bad enough to be insulted, but to hear the open and hostile disdain on a preference he'd done his best to deny and "cure" had only made it worse. He'd tried everything to be like the other men in his family and the academy and armada. To tell himself that he wasn't *really* gay. That it was a faze or curiosity. Or anything other than what it really was.

Only his fiancé, Tams, had made it bearable. Because she wasn't Phrixian, she'd assumed his strange behavior and reluctance to touch her was his own nervousness from being a different species.

Best of all, she'd given him an easy excuse to stay celibate. He'd told her that he didn't want to dishonor her before their wedding. Tams had thought it sweet, even while his father had rolled his eyes at something he considered unmanly. Phrixian males were slaves to their ids. Morality was dictated only when you went up against someone who could kick your ass. Otherwise, the universe was your playground and you did what you wanted.

The lies and unrelenting fear of being exposed had brought Maris one step shy of insanity.

Only Darling had known the truth and he'd coached Maris on how to fake a warrior's stride. On how to pass undetected around the staunch machismo that went against his natural tendencies. But for Darling and his help, Maris would have been killed before he reached his maturity. There was no such thing as a homosexual Phrixian. Never in his life had Maris met or even heard of anyone other than him.

And to be a prince on top of it. . .

That more than anything else was why his bounty was higher than Darling's or Nykyrian's. Nykyrian might have taken Kyr's eye, but so long as Maris lived, he was a blight on their family honor. And if one of his brothers could claim his life, he would be regaled by their parents for cleansing their gene pool. Maris's killer would be honored as a national hero.

A sudden flash to his right caught his attention.

Reacting on instinct, Maris dropped down an instant before a black dart sailed so close to his face, he felt the air burn of it. From behind, an assassin moved in with a knife as the crowd realized what was happening and panicked. People ran in all directions, screaming while they sought shelter. Maris spun and caught the man's wrist. The assassin cried out as Maris twisted and snapped the bone. The assassin came up with his blaster, but before he could fire it, Maris struck his nose with the heel of his hand. He wrested the blaster from the assassin's grip as the man fell to the street. Switching it to stun, Maris shot him and stayed low as he scanned for his next target.

He caught sight of the one who'd sent the dart at him and moved toward him with raw determination. Without realizing it, he fell into target fixation and missed the third assassin who sank a dagger deep into his side. Hissing, he turned and backhanded his assailant. As he moved to snap his neck, Maris froze.

Draygon. . .

His younger brother who was barely a year older than Saf.

He winced at the sight of him. Switching tactics, he held Draygon on the ground in a fierce grip against his neck. A smart man would end him. Brother or not. Yet when Maris went in for the kill, he didn't see a soldier.

He saw his brother laughing as they tried to jump over a ditch that had left Maris with a broken leg. Even though Draygon was injured himself, he'd carried Maris home.

This wasn't an enemy.

It was his little brother.

Draygon's dark eyes dared him now, just as they'd done as kids whenever they'd gotten crossed up over something. Maris could hear the taunt in his head. *Go ahead and hit me! I can take it.*

That was what they'd both been raised on.

Silent, Draygon stared defiantly, waiting for a death blow.

Maris jerked the dagger out of his injured side that Draygon had planted there. Without a word, he sank low and threw it straight into the heart of the assassin he'd been fixated on.

Still, his brother's gaze never wavered as he waited for Maris to kill him. Maris pinned him with a paralyzing hold that Draygon had never been able to escape. If Maris let him go, Draygon's honor would be eternally damaged. To be defeated by a target was the ultimate Phrixian insult.

For that target to be homosexual. . .

The kindest act would be to cut Draygon's throat and leave him dead on the street. But as Maris looked into a set of eyes identical to his own, he couldn't do it.

In spite of everything.

Knocking Draygon unconscious, he quickly moved away through the screaming civilians, with his hand pressed against his deep wound.

I have to get help. At the rate he was bleeding, he'd never make it to a hospital. He only had enough time for one call before he passed out, and most likely died in the street. . .

Without hesitating, he called the one single voice he needed to hear most.

"Hey, love. Are you on your way back?"

Maris panted with the weight of his pain as his vision

dimmed. "I'm badly wounded, Ture."

"What?"

Maris skirted into an alley and pressed his back to the stone wall as he slid down it, deeper into the shadows. He glanced around for more assassins. "I was attacked."

"Baby, where are you?"

Maris tried to focus, but warm blood kept flowing over his hand and down his leg. He slipped on it and hit the street.

"Mari! Talk to me."

"Um. . ." Everything spun around him. He tried to get up and couldn't. He was dying and he knew it. "Ture. . .I love you."

"MARIS!" TURE SHOUTED AS MARIS'S whispered words lanced his heart.

There was no answer.

Terrified as tears filled his eyes, he snatched off his apron and called Darling. He handed his apron to his sous chef. "You're in charge until I get back."

Her jaw dropped as he ran for the door. The moment Ture reached the street, Darling answered.

"Darling? It's Ture. Maris just called me and he's been attacked and is wounded. I think he passed out while he was talking to me. He didn't have a chance to tell me where he was. Help him, please. Tell me how to find him."

"Where are you?"

"I'm outside my restaurant."

He could hear the sounds of Darling running. "Okay. . . he left here about twenty minutes ago. He should be closer to the restaurant than the palace. He would have automatically gone for shelter. An alley probably. I'm on my way, but I have to hang up to trace him."

Tears streamed down Ture's face. "Find him, please." His breathing ragged as panic threatened to overtake him, he hung up and ran down Maris's route, trying to figure out where Maris might have gone.

By the fourth empty alley, he was ready to scream.

Please don't be dead. . .

Raw, unmitigated agony racked him. It was so consuming that he wanted to sink to his knees and scream out from the weight of it. Only the knowledge that Maris needed him kept him upright. He had to keep it together.

If Mari were here, he'd tell him to stay calm. To breathe.

As he reached the sixth alley, he heard the sounds of sirens. There were three bodies on the ground up ahead, and people gathered around them.

Closing the distance, he noticed drops of smeared blood on the sidewalk that stopped suddenly.

Maris. He must have realized he was leaving a trail.

Scared and shaking, Ture headed for the alley closest to the blood. He opened his mouth to call out then stopped himself. What if there were more attackers in the crowd? They might hear him and finish Maris off.

His entire body weak in fear and agony, he searched the alley for any telltale signs. He was just about to leave when he noticed a small red smear on a brick at his feet. Then he saw the heel of a dark maroon boot buried in debris. . .

"Mari," he breathed, running toward it.

Somehow, Maris had managed to tuck himself behind a small electrical unit. Careful not to hurt him, Ture pulled him out.

Oh God, no.

Blood saturated Maris's side. His face was pale with a bluish tint. Ture cradled him to his chest as he sobbed uncontrollably. "Don't you dare die on me, Mari! You hear me! Don't die. I can't live without you."

Suddenly, he heard someone running into the alley. Fearing it was an assassin, Ture grabbed Maris's reserve blaster from his boot and angled it toward the intruder.

Darling froze and held his hands up. "Don't shoot. It's the good guys."

Ture dropped it instantly. He couldn't speak as he

realized how much of Maris's blood was on him now. His lips trembled.

Darling and Hauk knelt by his side. He took Maris from Ture's arms and laid him flat on the ground. "I know you're going to hate me for this, Mari, but. . ." He ripped Maris's shirt and exposed the jagged wound in his side.

Opening a medical bag, Hauk called for Syn.

Ture struggled to contain his tears. The last thing he wanted to do was distract them with his useless hysteria. But it was so hard when inside he was screaming.

His hand trembling, he brushed the hair back from Maris's face while Darling and Hauk worked on him.

Darling cursed at the same instant Hauk's eyes widened with panic. He tilted Maris's head back and started chest compressions. "Breathe, damn you, breathe!" he growled.

All of a sudden, Syn was there with them.

Darling moved away and allowed him to take over. When Darling's agonized green gaze met Ture's, Ture saw just how much Maris meant to Darling, too.

In this fearful misery, they were kindred spirits.

"You stubborn Phrixian bastard. Pain in my ass," Syn snarled under his breath. "Don't you do this to us." He jerked an injector from his bag.

Ture's eyes widened at the size of it.

When Syn went to bury it in the center of Maris's heart, Ture started for him, but Darling caught him and held him back. "Don't look."

He couldn't take his eyes off them as Syn injected adrenaline directly into Maris's heart.

Just as Ture was about to scream, Maris took a deep, frantic breath and opened his eyes. Panting and shaking, Maris glanced around until he saw Ture with Darling. He held his hand out toward them.

At first, Ture thought he was reaching for Darling. But it was his fingers Maris's locked with. He pulled Ture closer until he could place a light, weak kiss to his knuckles.

More tears choked Ture as he returned to stroke Maris's hair while Syn stabilized him for mobility.

Darling sat by Ture's side and squeezed Maris's shoulder. "Next time you leave when I tell you not to, I swear I'll shoot you myself."

Maris coughed. "Just don't hit my groin."

"You're not funny," Ture and Darling said simultaneously.

Hauk laughed. "I think he's hilarious."

They both glared at him.

Aggravated to the extreme, Darling turned his back to Hauk as Maris nuzzled Ture's palm. It was only then that it dawned on Darling that Maris hadn't called *him* when he was hit.

He'd called Ture instead.

For one heartbeat, an insane stab of jealousy went through him. Since early childhood, Maris had been the one constant Darling could count on, no matter what. He'd had Mari to himself for so many years that it was hard to accept the fact that Maris finally had someone else.

Someone he loved enough that it had been Ture's voice alone that he'd wanted to hear before he died.

Not Darling's.

But that wasn't something to be jealous over. Maris deserved to be loved and cherished by someone who could give him everything he needed. And while Darling could give him his friendship and heart, he could never share his body with Maris. No matter how much he loved him.

For the first time, he fully understood the depth of Maris's love for him. Even though he was in love with him, Mari had tracked Zarya down and brought her back into Darling's life to heal his ravaged soul. How many people would be so altruistic?

Leaning down, Darling kissed Maris's bearded cheek. "Love you, Mari."

"Love you, too," Maris answered automatically. He smiled at Darling's heartfelt words until fear gripped him. He glanced up at Ture, expecting the worst.

There was no judgment or hatred in those beautiful gray eyes. No hesitancy in his touch as he continued to stroke Maris's hair.

Hauk went to meet the medics who were bringing in a stretcher for Maris.

Syn checked his vitals. "Barring infection, I think you're going to make it, bud. And don't you dare get an infection. This is as close to death as I want you to come in my lifetime."

Maris coughed. "I try to avoid Death as best I can. Bastard is relentless. I think he works for the League."

Ture and Darling stood up and moved back so that the medics could lift Maris onto the stretcher.

When they reached the transport, they both started to go in. Ture hesitated.

Darling smiled kindly. "Sorry. Habit. I know he'd rather have you with him."

Ture wasn't sure about that. Not that it really mattered right now. He dropped his gaze to Darling's blaster. "You should go. I can't protect him from another attacker. Not like you can. I'll meet you at the hospital."

His smile melted into a frown. "Are you sure?"

"Positive. This isn't about my ego. It's about Mari's life. Keep him safe for me. Please."

Darling hugged him before he climbed into the transport behind Syn.

"Don't worry," Hauk said as he draped an arm around Ture's shoulders. "I'll get you there before the transport."

MARIS PULLED THE MASK AWAY from his face as the transport took off. "Where's Ture?"

Darling returned it to his mouth and nose then held it in place so that Maris couldn't pull it off again. "He told me to go with you."

Wincing, Maris clenched his teeth. After all the times Ture had professed his love, Maris had never responded to it. But with Darling. . .

Maris hadn't even thought about it, or how it would

sound to Ture.

Damn. It had to cut deep. No wonder he'd stayed behind. His luck, Ture would never speak to him again.

"Shh," Syn said, leaning over him. "You need to calm down."

Easier said than done. He wouldn't have hurt Ture for anything.

What have I done?

When he failed to relax, Syn knocked him out.

TRUE TO HIS WORD, HAUK got Ture to the hospital on his airbike before the transport arrived. He was weak from fear over the way Hauk drove, but he was here in one piece. Physically, anyway.

Mentally was a whole other matter.

Hauk led him inside the lobby where Zarya, Princess Annalise, Drake and a man who looked a lot like Hauk was waiting for them. Zarya's pregnancy was now as evident as Ana's had been a few weeks ago.

Ture bit his lip as he saw how pale she appeared. "Are you okay, sweetie? Should you be standing?"

Her gaze flitted over the blood on Ture's clothes and skin as she paled even more. "Mari?" Her voice trembled.

"He's alive."

Closing her eyes, she sighed in relief and placed her hand to her heart. "I was terrified when Darling told me Maris had been ambushed. Are you okay?"

"Scared like you, but I'm not injured." Ture pulled her against him and held her close. "I've missed you."

"You, too." She leaned her head back to smile up at him. "Told you, didn't I?"

He rubbed his nose against hers. "Yes. You were right. I love Mari. He is everything you said, and then some."

Drake let out a low whistle to get their attention. "You let my brother see you molesting his wife like that, and I'll have to scrape your remains up with a spatula. No offense, I hate cleaning."

Zarya laughed. "Relax, Drake. Darling won't say a word."

Drake appeared highly doubtful as he moved to stand next to his sister, Annalise.

The doors opened. Ture turned to see the stretcher with Darling and Syn. Without pausing, Syn whisked Maris past him and through the ER doors.

Darling stopped by his side. "Mari's stable. He panicked when he realized I was with him and you'd stayed behind, so Syn knocked him out to keep his vitals at normal."

Ture sighed. "He is never going to believe that I'm not jealous of you. I don't know how to convince him that your relationship with each other doesn't bother me."

Darling arched a skeptical brow that was very similar to an expression Maris used. They'd known each other for so long that they shared many such quirks. "It doesn't?"

"No. Why should it? You've been in his life a lot longer than I have. It's not like you've slept with him or are going to. . .*that* I would issues with. Up until now, I've thought of you more like an irritating in-law Maris takes care of. . . one whose existence I have to suffer with in silence."

Darling's jaw went slack. "I think I'm insulted. . .And what do you mean *up until now*?"

Ture sobered. "He would have died today had you not been here. I could strangle him for calling me and not you. But for you, I would have had no idea where to look or any way to locate him. Thank you, Darling."

"You don't have to thank me for saving Mari. That's my job." Darling pulled Zarya into his arms to hold her. "Just take care of him for me. That's all I ask."

"Majesty?"

Darling turned as an officer joined them.

The male officer bowed low. "Two assassins were dead on arrival. The third killed three officers and escaped. We've notified all agencies to be on the lookout. Hopefully, we'll catch him."

Darling inclined his head. "Thank you for your service

and report."

The officer started to leave them then pulled his weapon out and angled it at the door.

Startled, Ture looked past him to see a uniformed League assassin entering the lobby. As soon as he saw the officer, he held his hands up and froze.

Darling pressed the man's blaster toward the floor. "It's all right, Officer Dalens. He's on our side."

Bowing again, the officer retreated.

Only then did the assassin approach. Tall, well-muscled, well-armed and raven-haired, he moved with the fluid grace of a lethal killer. Yet there was something strangely familiar about him.

"How is he?" the assassin asked Darling.

"He'll live. Any idea who got away from us?"

A tic started in the assassin's jaw. "Draygon. My guess is Mari let him go. There's no way Dray could have gotten away from him on his own. . .which means he's going on an asetum for the compassion."

"A what?" Ture asked.

Darling made a sound of supreme aggravation. "Blood vendetta to avenge his honor. But more serious than it sounds. When a Phrixian makes an asetum, it is to the death."

"In this case, Dray's. . .unless Mari lets him take his head. Stupid fucking bastard might do it, too."

Ture saw red at those words. Without thinking, he shoved the assassin back. "Don't you dare insult him!"

Darling came between them before the assassin could retaliate. "Emotions are running high here for all us. But before you two go at it, let me make introductions. Ture Xans meet Safir Jari. Saf is Maris's baby brother. Ture is the boyfriend."

That took the fight out of Ture, and the fire died in Saf's dark eyes.

"Sorry," they said at the same time.

So this was the brother that had been beaten in

Maris's stead.

The one Mari loved above all others.

By the slightly softened expression on Saf's face, Ture knew Maris had spoken to his brother about their relationship. But he wasn't quite sure what to make of it. Like all assassins, Saf kept his emotions visibly checked.

"I meant no disrespect to Mari," Saf explained. "He's just tender-hearted when it comes to our idiot brothers. Personally, I'd like to have a legal shot at Kyr. . .and most days, Dray, too."

"Yeah, but Dray's not League," Darling said. "The other two killed were."

Saf ground his teeth. "Kyr has called out the whole family on Maris so that we can avenge the shame he's brought to our house. Your little stunt at the prison killed the last shred of sanity Kyr possessed. While he'd love to have your head on his wall, it's Mari's he's obsessed with."

Ture scowled. "Why?"

The tic returned to Saf's jaw, something Mari's did whenever he was pissed off. "It would be bad enough if Maris was just gay. The fact he's gay and the best, most decorated warrior in our family. . .Kyr wants his testicles in a jar to prove he's the bigger man."

"Mari's better than you?" Ture couldn't help asking.

Safir went rigid. "I am damn good at what I do. I'd put my skills up against anyone's, any time, any place. . . except Maris's and Nykryian's." He glanced to Darling. "And the one man who taught Mari how to really fight, and blow shit to pieces. Growing up, I got into enough altercations with Mari to know he can sweep the floor with my ass, and that's with him holding back because he didn't really want to hurt me. While I can make him bleed, I can't stop him, and I know it. Unlike the rest of my family, I have a healthy respect and appreciation for my brother's abilities and skills."

Darling shrugged. "Yeah well, I learned most of what I know from Nyk."

"Which is why I'm not taking that contract. Or yours. I may be arrogant, but I'm not stupid. Luckily, Kyr and Dray hogged the family share of that."

Ture was beginning to really like Saf. Unlike the others of his ilk, Saf was strangely humble and kind.

Safir glanced around the room. "Speaking of, I better go. It wasn't exactly intelligent to come and be seen here. But when I heard Dray's report, I panicked and wanted to make sure he was lying about the severity of Mari's condition." He held his hand out to Darling.

"Peace, my brother." Darling took his hand then hugged him.

To Ture's complete shock, Saf pulled him into a full body embrace. "Take care of my brother for me. Tell him he can't die and leave me the sole source of sanity for the family. I'm depending on him to help me hold the line."

After giving Hauk the same hug he'd given Darling and kissing Zarya's cheek, Saf made a League sign of respect and solidarity over his heart then left.

Ture quirked a brow at Zarya. "He was unexpected."

She nodded. "I've loved Safir since the moment I met him. You know he's the only reason you and I are alive, right?"

Ture frowned. "No. How so?"

Darling crossed his arms over his chest. "After all of our combined resources failed to locate you, Saf's the one who found out where you were being held and got word to Maris. You'd both still be in prison, or dead, but for Safir."

Ture went cold at the courage that it took for Safir to go against Kyr and the rest of the League. If they ever learned what he'd done, they'd make sure his death was symbolic, painful and prolonged. "I like him all the more, now." He frowned. "Why didn't Maris tell me that?"

"Mari protects what he loves. It doesn't mean he doesn't trust you. But given his harsh upbringing, he's learned to say as little as possible when it comes to handing over information that could get someone killed. You've no idea the horrors of what he and Saf have been through. There's a reason their entire family is insane. And Maris is the sole reason Saf is halfway normal. He went out of his way to protect his brother, and show him that there were other ways to live than the severe life they'd been born to."

Ture digested that. "Mari never really talks about his family or past." Anytime he tried to broach the topic, Maris deftly changed subjects.

"Because it would break your heart." Darling led him away from the others so that they could talk in private. "Did you know that the Phrixians have thirty-three words for honor? Twenty for loyalty? Three dozen for betrayal, but not a single word for love?"

Ture gaped. "You're joking."

Darling shook his head slowly. "Their declaration of affection for one another is two words that translate to, *I will cause you no dishonor.* Or *esera diya kya, which means* I will die before I shame you. His people truly have no social concept of love."

"None?"

"Not even parent to child. Phrixian children are viewed as property of the government. Parents don't have them, nor do they raise them, because they want them or love them. They do so because it's their national duty to breed warriors to fight, and daughters to procreate the next generation of soldiers."

Horrified by what Darling described, he stared at him. "I can't even wrap my mind around what you're telling me."

"I know. Their world is mind boggling. Kids can be, and will be, taken from any parent who is deemed too lenient with them. At sixteen, their males are all conscripted into the military. Some girls, if they make the cut, can join, but it's frowned upon. There, they are viewed as government property until they're forty-two years old. Until then, they can't own anything or marry. Should they have a child, it's raised by the government and they know nothing of the child's upbringing."

"What happens to their daughters?"

Darling rolled his eyes in disgust. "If they're deemed beautiful or have the right lineage, they're put into the marriage pool as virgin trophies for the retiring warriors to choose a mate from. The rest become social servants, which includes servicing the conscripted soldiers whenever they earn sex privileges."

Ture frowned. "I'm confused. Mari was engaged and had property at one time. He's told me that much."

"Maris is a prince. While they still have to abide by the same laws as everyone else, they, alone, are allowed to own property before they leave military service, and can marry should their father need them for a political match. Even married, they still can't live with their wife until they turn forty-two and are released from service. The only other honorable way out, for any of them, is to be good enough to join the League as assassins, such as Saf and Kyr."

Where they were forced to be celibate, and where no one could retire. Assassins were killed the moment they became too old or too injured to continue their duties.

Tears filled Ture's eyes as he tried to imagine how horrible that existence had been for his peace-loving Maris. "Mari said that the League forced his father to give up one son to mix with humans."

Darling nodded. "Maris was a political prisoner for ten years."

Ture narrowed his gaze at Darling. "Prisoner? From the way he explained it, I thought he was just fostered by a human family."

Darling let out a bitter, angry laugh. "I so love how Mari sugarcoats things for the ones he loves." His gaze seared Ture. "He was barely five, and couldn't understand a single word of Universal or any language other than Phrixian, when his own father handcuffed him and surrendered him to League custody with one order. . .You bring any shame to Phrixus and we'll dine on your liver."

Nauseated, Ture stared at him. “What?”

Glancing back toward Zarya, Darling sighed heavily. “His father wasn’t joking. He would have killed Mari had he received any report of misbehavior or problems. So there was Mari, with no understanding of kindness or love or compassion of any kind, unable to comprehend what the foreign people around him were saying, thrown to the wolves. Alone.”

As little more than an infant.

And Darling made no mention of Mari’s amphibious nature and the stress of keeping *that* secret. Even though he abhorred violence, Ture wanted to kill Maris’s family for the cruelty of abandoning a boy so young.

“On Phrixus,” Darling continued, “anyone does anything you don’t like, you two fight until one of you loses consciousness or dies. That is the Prime Law. Suddenly, Maris was thrown into a world where he was forbidden to strike out at all. For any reason. Everything he’d been trained and taught from birth was the exact opposite of what was expected of him once he left Phrixian territory. He had to curb every instinct he possessed or die for it. The League told him he better not even swat and kill a fly or they’d retaliate. First against him. Then his people.”

Ture’s stomach cramped at the horror Maris must have felt as a small child, alone in a world he didn’t understand. “Where did he live?”

“The League handed him over to the Ultaran royal family.”

Ture wasn’t sure where Ultara was, but he knew the name of the planet. “Why there?”

“The Ultarans had been at war with the Phrixians for centuries. No one cared about it, until a League convoy was caught in the crossfire. Sincc the Phrixians were the ones who blew it apart, they were punished more severely than the Ultarans. The League High Command demanded that the Phrixian emperor hand over a son for a decade to the Ultarans to guarantee a cease fire between their empires.”

"And the Ultarans? What was their punishment?"

"They basically skated with a slap on their wrist."

Ture was disgusted by how the League operated. "So Mari was handed over to his father's enemies?"

The expression on Darling's face confirmed Ture's fears. "He was."

And as the son of their enemy. . ."I take it they weren't kind."

"You know how I met Maris, right?"

It was one of Mari's favorite memories. "You saved him from a bully."

"The Ultaran prince. Crispin. I'll admit I was scared as hell that day. It was the first time I'd ever been away from home or family, and all I wanted was for the day to end and for my dad to come get me." Darling paused as the memory played through his mind. Even all these years later, he could see it as if it'd been yesterday.

He'd been playing tag with another boy when Crispin, who dwarfed both him and Maris, threw Maris on the ground and held him there by his hair. Maris's eye was cut and his nose bleeding from the punches Crispin had already given him.

"You're not so tough, are you, Phrixian? You're nothing but a puss. Say, I'm a scared little bitch. Say it!"

A group of older boys, Crispin's friends, were circled around them and laughing about Maris's abuse.

"Say it, Phrixian scum!"

If Darling lived a thousand years, he'd never forget the fear he saw on Maris's face.

Because of Darling's father, who often attended sessions and meetings with Darling on his lap, Darling was well advanced in politics for his young age, and he'd known who Maris was and why he was at their school. Most of all, he'd known that Maris was forbidden to defend himself. If he dared fight back, a report would have been filed with the League, and Maris would have been executed for it. If not by the League or Ultarans then by his own father.

Maris had said something in Phrixian, but Darling's understanding of the language at that time had been as poor as Maris's of theirs.

"What?" Crispin had shouted in his ear. "You want to suck my dick? Is that what you said, you freak?" He rose with his hand still wrapped in Maris's hair.

Because he'd already started military training before he'd been handed over to the League, Maris had feinted to the right then reversed course. And even though he'd left a clump of bloody hair in Crispin's hand, he'd shot across the yard with the others giving chase.

Two of the older students had tripped him as he ran past them. With a fluid grace, Maris had rolled and sprung to his feet. But no sooner had he regained his footing than Crispin slammed him against the wall and started pounding on him again.

Darling had looked at their teachers who were ignoring it. They knew Crispin's father would only punish them if they intervened. As an emperor, he had total power over them. And since Maris's father wouldn't do anything to help his son, they refused to render aid and risk their own necks or jobs.

Unable to stand another minute of the cruelty, Darling had shot across the yard and slammed his body into Crispin's, knocking him away from Maris. Blinded by fury, Darling had beat the shit out of the sniveling coward.

Twice his size and age, Crispin had cried like an infant.

"Swear to me that you won't hit him anymore! Ever!" Darling had demanded.

"No!"

Darling had punched him, again and again, until his own knuckles were bleeding and bruised. "Swear it! Or so help me, I'll beat you every time I see you!"

"Okay! I swear I won't ever hit him again."

"Not even at home!"

"Not even at home."

Only then had Darling pulled back. Aching and winded,

he'd turned around to see Maris still against the wall, staring at him as if afraid Darling would take over where Crispin had left off.

Darling had smiled at him and tried to think of something Maris would understand in Universal. "Hi, I'm Darling Cruel. We should be friends."

Maris had frowned as he struggled to translate what Darling was saying.

So Darling had pulled his hand-sized notepad from his pocket, and downloaded a translator to say it to him in Phrixian.

Only then did Maris return his smile. He'd reached for the notepad and typed in a response. "Your services were necessary and memorized."

It would be months before Darling understood the strangeness of that comment. Phrixians had no words for friend, gratitude or thank you.

He'd pointed to himself. "Darling."

Maris had done the same. "MAH-ress"

From that moment forward, Darling had kept Maris close, watching his back while he taught Mari Universal and Mari taught him Phrixian well enough that they could talk to each other fluently. Those days had been so hard for Maris. Darling couldn't even count how many times Maris had come to school with bruises and cuts from where the Ultarans had attacked him when he was on their soil.

Mari never said a word about it. Nor did he try to befriend anyone else. *I am loyal to you, alone, Darling.* They *are untrusted.*

His mistrust had only grown when he saw how viciously their classmates had turned on Darling when Darling, to save his mother's life for an affair that would have seen her executed, had claimed her male lover as his. After that, Maris had never trusted anyone with anything about him that could cause harm to his body or heart.

It was why the two of them were closer than brothers.

Why Darling could kill anyone who caused harm to Maris.

Darling's thoughts returned to the present as he stared into Ture's eyes. In all these years, Ture was the only one Maris had ever given his heart to.

That alone told him how much Maris loved Ture. "As scared as I was, I knew Maris was even more so. And I couldn't stand by and watch him be hurt."

"You're a good man, Darling."

He scoffed at Ture's praise. "Not really. Flawed like everyone else. But I try. And I'm just grateful that Crispin went to the same academy I did, otherwise I'd have never met Maris. And I shudder at what would have become of us had we not found each other. I know I wouldn't have made it through without him."

"He feels the same way about you, Darling. And now I understand exactly why. I can't imagine how awful that had to be for him."

"Yeah, it was harsh. While the rest of us went home for holidays and breaks, Maris couldn't. His family was only allowed to visit with League chaperones, and only for a few hours at a time. Which they very seldom did." And then it was only to threaten him. "Meanwhile, after our regular classes ended, he spent another six hours a day with Phrixian tutors who continued his lessons that contradicted everything our academy drilled into him. Talk about homework. . .You can't imagine the workload he carried, and he wasn't allowed to slack off or do badly in any subject, either human or Phrixian."

"Why not?"

"Honor. To fail or allow a human to outdo him would shame his family. He would go days without sleeping, just so that he could keep up."

Ture winced. No wonder Maris seldom tired, and never complained about staying the long hours they did at the restaurant. He was used to it. "Did he never get a break?"

"Sometimes. Because of our friendship, my father intervened as best he could between the League, Phrixians and Ultarans so that Maris would be allowed to stay with us, or visit. For seven years, we did a pretty good job running interference."

"Only seven?"

Darling's eyes turned dark with grief. "My father was assassinated when I was twelve. And though some of the loopholes he'd set up for Mari that allowed him to visit remained, my uncle wanted me isolated. He made it clear that he'd rather Maris stay away. So for two and a half years, he was left at the academy without me. It's something he never talks about, so I know it had to be bad for him."

"And after that he went into the Phrixian armada."

Darling nodded. "That, too, was a nightmare for him. Because he'd been 'humanized' by something he'd been forced to do against his will, the Phrixians went out of their way to punish him for it. They perceived him as weak and tainted by his time with the Ultarans. It's why his father chose a non Phrixian to marry him. He didn't want Maris shaming his family with his human sympathies and effeminate ways. Nor did he want one of his other 'pure' sons tainted by the stench of a human."

"How did Maris stand it?"

Darling laughed bitterly. "Mostly, he lashed out. He was angry all the time back then. Furious at his father, his family. Sometimes even me. It was what made him such a great warrior. He'd unleash that fury and beat the hell out of anyone who got near him."

Ture drew a ragged breath as he finally understood the two contradictory sides of Maris's personality, and how he could swing from flirting to vicious killer so fast. "You know, I used to hate you so much. I spent countless hours cursing everything about you and your royal family. Wishing you were all dead and gone. . .I'm sorry, Darling. I shouldn't have judged you or hated you, when I knew nothing about your character or situation. And I can't thank you enough for everything you've done for Maris. I totally get his devotion now."

Darling gave him a sad smile. "Maris and I have been to hell and home together. Back to back, we have defended each other with everything we possess. Anytime we needed to turn to someone, we called each other. Until today. When he thought he was dying, it was your voice he wanted to hear last. Not mine. Honestly, a part of me is a little hurt. I've never had to share him before with anyone. But I love him enough to let him go. His happiness means everything to me."

"Me, too."

Darling hugged him close. "Thank you for calling me."

"Thank you for saving him."

He pulled back and offered his hand to Ture. "Brothers?"

"Brothers."

MARIS CAME AWAKE TO A searing pain in his side. Grimacing, he opened his eyes to find Syn checking the bandage over his ribs. As he realized he was in a hospital, everything came rushing back to him.

The attack.

Draygon. . .

And Ture refusing to get into the ambulance after Maris had told Darling he loved him.

Shit. The fallout was bound to be nuclear.

Syn jerked his head up to meet his gaze as Maris tried to speak. "Easy, Mari. I've got you locked down."

Unable to speak, he used his one free hand to sign to Syn.

"Darling's outside with the others."

Maris had just started asking about Ture when the bathroom door opened, and Ture drew up short.

"He's awake?"

Syn nodded. "He just opened his eyes."

Ture rushed to the opposite side of the bed. Leaning over the rail, he smiled at Maris as he brushed his hand through his hair. "Hey, baby. You gave us all a big scare."

Confused, Maris tried to make sense of this. He'd expected Ture's anger.

Not his love.

Syn pulled the mask off his face then handed him a small glass of water. "Sip slowly."

Ture helped him with it.

Maris coughed then met Ture's gray eyes. "You're not mad at me?"

"For what? Getting stabbed? I don't think you did it on purpose, did you?"

"No. . .for Darling."

Ture duplicated his frown. "For Darling what?"

"For what I said to him."

Now he looked irritated. "That you loved him?"

Maris nodded.

Ture rolled his eyes. "Why would I get angry over that? I know you love him. It's not like you *ever* kept that a secret."

"Then why didn't you get in the ambulance?"

His features softened as he brushed his hand over Maris's face. "I was afraid you'd be attacked again, love. I wanted men with you who know how to butcher something besides a steak."

"Really?"

Ture sighed heavily. "I am *not* jealous of you and Darling, Mari. How many times do I have to say that before you believe me? I would never come between the two of you, and what you've shared. And in the future, when you're dying, for the love of the gods, please call the one capable of saving your life and not the one who can't."

Maris laced his fingers with Ture's. "You are my life."

Ture smiled at him as he lifted his hand to his lips and kissed his knuckles. "I feel the same way about you, which is why I want to beat you for calling me when you should have called an ambulance." He glanced over to Syn. "So how's he doing, Doc?"

"Better." He locked gazes with Maris. "You still took one hell of a stab, though. Your brother nicked your artery and went straight into your intestines. Recovering from it is going to hurt."

"What can I say? Dray's good at what he does. I didn't even see him until he had me."

Syn curled his lip. "Don't praise that bastard to me. I want his heart in my fist. And speaking of. . ." He began detaching the monitors from Maris's body. "You'll do better if we can get you into the tub for a little while. I'm going to assume you'd prefer Ture help you with that."

"If you don't mind, I would."

A smile broke across Syn's face. "Well, as much as I love seeing you naked, Mari, I'll gladly surrender you to your boyfriend."

Maris arched a brow at those words. It was the first time ever that Syn had teased him like that. Normally, he was the one harassing Syn. He'd respond to it, but the last thing he wanted was for Ture to take him seriously and get his feelings hurt. Syn pulled back. "You want to try and walk or should I call someone?"

"I'll walk."

"All right. Give me a few minutes to run the water and I'll be back." He headed for the bathroom.

Ture lowered the rail and sat on the edge of Maris's bed. "They shaved your beard off."

"I'm sorry. I'll grow it back for you."

Tears filled Ture's eyes at those words. "For what it's worth, I don't ever want to feel like this again, Mare. When the line went silent and I thought you were dead. . ." A single tear ran down his cheek. "I haven't hurt like that since my baby sister died. And what I felt when I thought you were dead made a mockery of even that."

Maris pressed his lips together to keep from smiling. "I feel terrible that I scared you. That I hurt you, but. . ." He let his smile loose. "I do love you, Ture."

"I love you, too. But don't ever die on me."

"I have no intention of it."

Ture carefully laid his body against Maris's and held him. Pulling back, he wiped at his tears. "By the way, the size of your family scares me."

"What do you mean?"

"You should see how many people are outside. It's ridiculous. Darling, his two brothers, his sister. Zarya and Sorche. Fain and Hauk have positions at the door and won't let any medical staff other than Syn in here without them standing over them. And they run every badge before the let them in. Nykyrian and his wife and their oldest daughter and one of their sons. Syn's wife and son, and her two sisters, and Caillen. His wife and their daughter. Chayden and his friend. Jayne and her husband and three kids. Nero. And Safir keeps checking in. All of them are desperate to see you and know how you're doing."

"And the most important one is sitting right here."

Ture smiled. "I love it when you sweet talk me."

"All right," Syn said as he returned. "Let's get you submerged."

Ture moved aside so that Syn could help him to the tub. Then Syn surrendered custody to Ture.

"There's a link right here." Syn showed it to Ture. "If you need anything, call. I'll be back in a little bit to check on him."

"Thank you, Syn," they said simultaneously.

He inclined his head and left.

Maris lay back against the tub and sighed as the water soothed him. He frowned as he caught the odd look on Ture's face. "What?"

"Your eyes turn silver even when your head isn't in water."

"I know."

"It's just so strange to me that it doesn't pain you to change. It seems like it should."

Maris shrugged. "I never think about it." He brushed Ture's hair back from his eyes. "How long have I been out?"

"Three days."

He gasped at the length of time. "What time is it?"

Ture checked his watch. "Early evening. Little after seven."

"Shouldn't you be at the restaurant?"

"You know here's the funny thing. . .I don't want to leave you. I don't care if the restaurant burns to the ground right now."

"Ture—"

He placed his fingers over Maris's lips, cutting off his words. "It's true. I went yesterday to close up and. . .it felt so empty without you there. I kept expecting to see you at my desk or in the doorway. You've absolutely ruined me, Mari. I should shoot you for that."

Maris took his hand into his and stared at them entwined. His skin shimmered with its peculiar silver hue against Ture's dark, tawny flesh. "I can't believe I finally found you."

"Just make sure you keep me."

Maris smiled, but underneath his happiness was the fear of what was coming for them. Dray wouldn't rest until he was dead. Neither would Kyr.

In the past, he hadn't cared. But Ture was a weakness he'd never had before. Today, he was the one in the hospital.

But what if Ture had been with him? What if Dray, out of sheer cruelty, had gone for Ture's life?

How would he live with himself if he caused the one person he loved above all others to die?

He didn't say that out loud, but in his heart, he knew the truth. Somehow he was going to have to find the courage to walk away.

Before his brothers killed them both.

Chapter 11

THIS HAD BEEN THE LONGEST week of Ture's life. What none of them had known was that Dray's knife had been coated with a slow-acting poison that had sent Maris into seizures. Had anyone other than Syn been his attending physician, Maris would have died.

They finally had him out of danger and resting.

But Ture couldn't shake the image of Maris flat-lining. If he ever laid hands to Dray, he, the pacifist, was going to cut out his heart, sauté it with onions, and feed it to Kyr.

He heard his link buzzing. Answering it, he smiled at the image of Mari in his hospital bed. "Hey, handsome."

"Hi, gorgeous. Are you at the restaurant yet?"

"Walking in now." Ture slid in through the backdoor. He still hated that he'd allowed Maris to talk him into returning so soon. Had it been left up to him, he would have stayed with Maris until Syn cleared him to return home. But Ture had made one condition. He would only return to work if Mari came with him.

Ture sent the link transmission to the large monitor on the wall at the same time his staff bombarded him with questions about Maris's health. "See for yourselves, he's on his way to full recovery." Ture grinned at Maris. "Told you they missed you, too."

Maris laughed. "Hi, everyone."

Ture stood back as his staff took turns chatting with Maris while they got ready for the dinner rush. He hadn't realized how much his staff had embraced Maris as part of their eclectic family until Mari had been injured. In a very short time, Mari had come to mean a lot to all of them.

Anachelle gasped as she came in the backdoor and saw the monitor. She rushed forward with Terek and waved his little hand at Maris. "Hey, Uncle Mari Daddy! We tried to visit, but they wouldn't let your son in. He's too young."

Maris's eyes widened. "Look how big he's gotten. Ah! I wish I could hold him."

Ture laughed as Maris baby-talked to the bald infant who stared at him with an adorable expression of total confusion.

When Terek started crying, Ana excused herself to change him.

Ture stepped forward. "All right, everyone, we need to focus and get ready. Maris will stay with us while he's awake so ignore him like we always do when he's really here."

His sous chef, Amberlia, laughed. "Only you ignore him when he's here. The rest of us actually talk to him."

"It's true," Maris said with a wicked grin. "You only talk to me when you want to use me as a guinea pig."

Ture arched a brow at him. "Play nice. I do have a switch I can turn you off with."

A light came into those dark eyes that let him know Maris had a sexual comment to make over that, but bit it back. *That's why I love you, so.*

His fierce warrior was ever a gentleman.

MARIS TUCKED HIS ARM BEHIND his head as he watched Ture and his staff work. Until now, he hadn't realized how much he missed being with them. He'd searched everywhere for a place to belong. But in all his wildest imaginings, he'd never dreamed it would be in a commercial kitchen.

The door to his room opened.

He muted his mic as he looked up to find Darling moving toward the bed.

"How are you feeling?"

"Good."

"Then what's wrong?"

Maris looked away. He knew better than to try and hide his feelings from Darling. A thousand images went through his head as he thought about all the times in his past when he'd needed someone, and Darling had appeared as if he'd sensed Maris's pain. "I don't know what to do."

"About?"

"Ture."

Darling sat on the edge of the bed and pinned him with a hard stare. "I don't think I understand the question. You love him, so. . ."

"I endanger him." Maris swallowed hard against the lump in his throat. "Over and over, I keep seeing you when Nykyrian told you that Zarya was dead. I feel how you shook in my arms, and the ragged, raw pain in your eyes. I really get it now."

Darling took his hand into his. "It's scary as hell. Honestly, I don't know how Nyk copes with Kiara being a civ. With Zarya, I know she's trained to defend herself and to kill any attacker. Still, with her pregnant, she can't do that and every second of every minute, I'm a nervous wreck. I just want to tie her to me and make sure that nothing bad ever happens to her again, and I can only imagine how much worse that's going to be when my son's born and I have him to worry over, too. But what choice do we have?"

"We leave."

"Mare-bear. . .you did not just say that to me."

Maris sniffed back his tears at the teasing nickname Darling hadn't used since they were kids. "I don't like feeling this way. You know my brothers, Dar. They would be giddy with joy if they could lay hands on Ture."

"I know. Kyr is as much a threat to me as he is to you. But you and Ture can move into the palace where we have round–the-clock surveillance, and a full military guard. I'll assign him the best of my guard staff. Even Sentella if you want. He can have them full time."

"Gods, I love you."

"I love you, too, Mari. There's nothing I wouldn't do for you, you know that. And what can I say? Being in love sucks. Life's hard enough when you only have to worry about your own ass. When there's someone else whose life means even more to you. . .They have you by the stones."

"You sound like Drake."

"Yeah, I think the little bastard's starting to rub off on me. Since you've been spending so much time with Ture, you've forced me to start actually talking to my brother. I owe you a serious ass-beating for that."

He laughed. "You love Drake."

"In small doses." Darling leaned forward as he finally noticed the small tablet on Maris's tray table. "What's that?"

Maris turned it toward him so that he could see the kitchen. "Ture refused to go to work unless I went with him. This way, we can keep an eye on each other."

Darling waved at Ture who still couldn't hear them. Smiling, Ture waved back then ran to put out a small pan fire. "I always knew you'd fall for a cook."

"Yeah, I know." Maris drew a ragged breath as he returned the tray to its original position. "Thanks, Darling. I appreciate the talk."

"Not sure I did anything."

"You did what you always do, gave me hope. And you talked sense to me."

"Anytime, brother."

Maris felt the familiar sad emptiness as Darling let go of his hand and left the room. He'd never really thought any other man could make him feel that sensation.

Not until Ture.

Turning the sound on, he moved his hand so that he could trace the line of Ture's jaw while he went around the kitchen with unparalleled grace. He could watch that man move all day long. Nothing gave him more pleasure.

How can I even think about leaving him?

But the real question was—how could he endanger him by staying?

Ture froze as he glanced at the monitor and caught the unguarded expression on Mari's face. For a full minute, he couldn't move for it. No one had ever looked at him like that.

Like he was the air Maris breathed.

I feel the same way about you, baby.

And the last thing he wanted was to be here tonight without him. He missed being with Maris more than he would have ever thought possible. Even though he could see Maris on the monitor, it wasn't the same as stealing a quick kiss from him as he passed by. Of Maris walking up behind him for a drive-by hug while Ture held a spoon out for Maris to taste what he was working on. . .

Love you, he mouthed at the screen.

You, too, Maris mouthed back.

"Ture?"

He turned at Ana's voice. "Yes, sweetie?"

"Can I lay T in your office while he naps?"

"Of course. I had a small crib put in there yesterday for him." Since she'd been running things for him again while he stayed with Maris, he'd thought it the best way to make her and the baby more comfortable.

She gaped at him. "Did you really?"

"Of course. Least I could do for my boyfriend's son."

Laughing, she rolled her eyes. "Remind me later that I have the custody papers for Maris to sign in my diaper bag. They came in today and you can take them up to the hospital later."

"Will do, sweetie." He turned back to Maris. "You're about to be childless again, hon."

Maris pouted. "Tell Ana I still want visitation rights to my boy."

"I'm sure she'll let us babysit." Ture paused as he saw Maris bite back a yawn. "Are you tired?"

"I'm good."

He narrowed his gaze on him. "Turn it off and go to sleep. I'll be back as soon as we close."

The reluctance in those dark eyes touched him deeply. "I'd rather stay with you."

"As would I, but I don't think you want everyone to know what a loud Snore-a-saurus you are."

Maris laughed. "I don't snore. You do."

"Hmm-mmm, go on and believe the lies you tell."

"Fine. I'm going. I'll see you later, sweetie."

Ture blew him a kiss before he shut the feed off. But as he did so, a wave of tears choked him as he felt Maris's absence like a physical ache. *It's just a few more hours.* He'd lived most of his life without Maris in it. So why was this so hard now? In the past, he'd been eager to have time alone. While he'd enjoyed his time with his boyfriends, he'd also needed time to himself every so often.

He never felt that with Mari. The more he was with him, the more he had no desire to be alone. Ever. He wanted to share everything with Maris.

It made no sense, but he couldn't deny what was in his heart.

Trying to put it out of his mind, he forced his thoughts to cooking and running his restaurant.

"IS HE STILL ASLEEP?"

Ana nodded as she rejoined Ture at the sink. "I just checked to make sure he was breathing. He's never napped this long before. But he seems fine. Granted, it's weird and unnerving."

"Guess he was tired." He finished rinsing out the sink. "Did you get the orders entered?"

"All done. You?"

He wiped his hands on his towel then pulled his apron off. "Done. Finally."

"Then I'll go get Terek and we can call it a night." She took a step away from him and froze.

Ture opened his mouth to ask what was wrong, but the words choked him as he saw three uniformed League assassins with his brother.

Bristol tsked at him. "I finally realized why your current boyfriend looked so familiar to me, and why neither of you would tell me his name. . .Maris Sulle. He must be able to suck the plating off a starship for you to not give him up for the credits his ass is worth."

Dread tore through Ture at those words and what his brother had obviously done. "Tell me you didn't."

"I did, and you should have given me the money I asked for, Ture. It would have saved us both a lot of trouble."

Chapter 12

Maris jerked awake in his bed. "Ture?"

"Darling."

He turned to see Darling sitting in the chair Ture often slept in. "What time is it?"

"Just after one."

He went cold with that answer. "Where's Ture?"

"Is he supposed to be here?"

"Yeah. He was coming over after closing. He should have been here hours ago." Maris started to climb out of bed, but Darling caught him.

"Don't panic. Call him." Darling handed him his link.

Maris made the call.

There was no answer. His breathing ragged, he met Darling's worried gaze as he tried to call Anachelle who'd been closing with Ture.

Again, no one picked up.

His panic grew even more. "He wouldn't have gone home, Dar. And even if he had, he would have answered my call."

"Okay. You stay here in case they're on their way, and I'll go check the restaurant and his apartment."

Maris desperately wanted to go with him, but Darling

was right. He needed to stay in case they were in a low reception area while en route to the hospital. Satellites occasionally malfunctioned and went down. . .

It could be nothing. Terek might have gotten sick and they could be at a twenty-four hour pediatric clinic with him,

"Please hurry."

Darling inclined his head to him. "You know I will. I'll call as soon as I get there."

Maris nodded as Darling left. Hauk came in a second later.

"What are you doing here?"

Hauk grinned. "Sitting on you while you panic. Making sure you don't do something stupid. Are you planning to be stupid?"

"I try to avoid it."

"Good for you. I don't. Rather I embrace my natural stupidity with both arms."

In spite of his panic, Maris laughed. He loved the grouchy Andarion. Hauk was always worth his weight in laughter. But still, he was worried. "They're okay, right, Hauk?"

"Of course. You know we're not going to let anything happen to your family."

Maris was desperate to believe that. But as he waited to hear from Darling, he cursed himself for ever turning the monitor off. How could he have gone to sleep and left Ture alone?

Please be all right. . .

He'd never forgive himself if something had happened while he slept.

Time dragged until he finally saw Darling calling him. He picked up and heard a baby crying in the background. "Is that Terek?"

"Yeah."

His stomach pitched as Darling fell silent and he heard nothing other than the baby. "What is it?"

"Is Hauk with you?"

This was bad. . .

"I'm right here. Why?"

"I need you to hold on to Mari for me."

"What!" Maris snarled. "Darling, tell me what the fuck's going on."

When he finally spoke, his voice was tense and deep. "Anachelle is dead in the kitchen, and it's obvious there was a bad fight here."

"Ture?"

"No sign of him. By the looks of it, I think he was taken."

Maris couldn't breathe as those words slapped him hard.

"Terek seems to be fine. For some reason, they left him in his crib in Ture's office. I've already got everyone on this and Jayne's taking Terek home with her while we mobilize. We will find him, Mari, you know we will."

But in what condition?

Terror consumed him. It was so foul and biting that it made his ears buzz. His sight dimmed as his blood rushed thick and hard through his veins. He locked gazes with Hauk. "Get your hands off me or lose them."

"Maris—"

"Hauk. . .have you ever seen what a Phrixian can do when cornered?"

"Maris, don't!" Darling snapped.

"If this was Zarya?"

Darling cursed. "Let him go, Hauk. He's right. As badass as you are, in the mood Mari's in, you'd need backup. Phrixians are like rabid animals when wounded. They're three times as strong as normal, and don't feel pain until their adrenaline stops rushing. Think of Nykyrian with a shot of Prinam in him."

And right now, Maris felt nothing except the desire to rip the throat out of whoever was dumb enough to take Ture from him.

Hauk stepped back then gaped as Maris pulled the monitors off and stood without flinching. Like Darling said, he felt no pain and wouldn't until he calmed again.

He headed to the bag Ture had brought from home and

dressed. The last time Maris had felt like this was when the Resistance had kidnapped Darling. He'd been insane until they found him.

As soon as he was dressed, he returned to Hauk and stripped him of his weapons. Hauk didn't say a word or try to stop him. He merely handed them over, one by one.

"You're going to need a ride."

Maris strapped the blaster to his hips. "I'll drive."

Hauk hesitated. "You suck at driving."

"So do you."

He flashed a fanged grin then surrendered his keys. "Oh yeah, I do."

Maris headed out with Hauk and Fain flanking him. He was going to find Ture, and he planned to tear anyone with his boyfriend into small, bloody pieces.

Chapter 13

Ture watched the blood dripping from his nose and mouth as it splattered against the white floor beside the chair he was tied to. He hurt so badly, he couldn't draw a breath without his eyes tearing up.

The League officer buried a gloved hand in his hair and snatched his head back so that Ture was forced to stare up at the bastard. "Either tell us where he is or call him!"

"Fuck you."

The soldier backhanded him again. "Answer the question, you stupid faggot!" He struck him again.

Ture laughed. "I might be gay, but you're the one who's going to get publicly butt-fucked when Maris gets here. He'll tear all of you apart for what you've done." For the first time in his life, he believed that. He had no doubt that Maris would come for him.

The soldier hit him again and again. Finally, he pulled back. "Had enough yet?"

Ture scoffed. "You hit like a girl. Who taught you to fight? Your decrepit grandmother?"

Shrieking, the League soldier kicked his chair, knocking him over. Ture groaned as pain slammed through his entire body.

"I'm sick of this." The other assassin opened the door and spoke to someone in the hallway. "Bring his brother in here."

While they waited, the assassins set him back up in the chair. Blood suffused his mouth as his vision dimmed. They'd been at this for hours. It was like being held with Zarya all over again, except this time he did know the answer they wanted.

But he'd die before he gave them Maris.

The first round of torture had been water and electrocution. Then they'd moved to drugs and purges. Choking.

Now, an old-fashioned beating.

None of it mattered as he finally understood how Zarya had managed to go through everything without speaking. And to think he'd criticized her for it.

He'd laugh at the irony if it didn't hurt so much to breathe.

Another League soldier brought Bristol into the cell and forced him on his knees in front of Ture. His hands were cuffed behind his back and someone had gagged him. Eyes wide with fear, he tried to say something to Ture, but he couldn't understand a single word.

The soldier who'd done most of the beating, pulled his blaster out and angled it at Bristol's head. "Now answer the question or I'm going to paint the wall with your brother's brain matter."

Bristol screamed against his gag.

Ture's stomach heaved at the threat. Time stopped as he stared into the same eyes his sister had held, and he remembered holding her hand while she took her last breath. The shrill sound of the monitors flat-lining was forever engraved in his heart. Bristol had just been a boy and Ture had held him for hours as he cried.

The assassin removed Bristol's gag.

Tears fell down his cheeks as he sobbed. "P-p-please, Ture. Don't let them hurt me!"

It was the same plea Anachelle had made.

Completely unsympathetic, Bristol had curled his lip at her. *"Shut that bitch up."*

They had shot her a heartbeat later. The horror of seeing her die for no reason sickened him. The fact that his own brother had told them to silence her. . .

Unforgivable.

"I love you, Bristol," Ture whispered.

Bristol smiled. "Then tell them where Sulle is. We can split the reward. You and me! It's a fortune, Ture. We can both retire. We'll never have to work again."

Hot tears stung the cuts on his face as they fell. Ture drew a ragged breath and shook his head. "Sorry. I love Mari more."

"I'm your brother!"

And Maris was his heart.

The League soldier sank his hand into Bristol's hair and pressed the tip of the blaster to his temple. "I *will* do this."

Ture had no doubt. Killing people was their specialty. "I know."

"Ture. . .you can't let me die."

"I didn't do this, Bristol. You did." Had Bristol not called the League, wanting to claim the bounty on Maris's life, they wouldn't be here now.

"They're going to kill me, big brother! Please help me!"

Ture screamed out as agony ripped him apart. He didn't want to do this. What kind of monster consigned his own brother to death?

"One last time, cock-jockey. Where's Sulle?"

Before he could even draw his breath, the door behind the soldier blew apart.

"I'm right here, asshole." Maris opened fire on him and then swung his blaster to the other two in the room. Before Ture could blink, they were dead.

Ignoring Bristol, Maris ran to Ture and knelt beside his chair. His hand shaking, he brushed the hair back from Ture's battered face. "Baby?"

"I knew you'd find me."

Maris cut his restraints and pulled him into his arms as Darling joined them in the room. "Thank the gods you're alive."

"What about this one?" Hauk asked as he covered Bristol with his blaster. "Friend or foe?"

Maris helped Ture to his feet. "Ture?"

"He's my brother."

Hauk cut Bristol free while Maris leaned Ture against the wall and inspected his wounds.

Darling checked the corridor for more League soldiers.

Maris clicked on his link. "Caillen? Report?"

"I think we got them all on the way in. You should be free to the shuttle."

Maris held his hand out to Ture. To his complete shock, Ture grabbed the reserve blaster from his hip and angled it up. Stunned, he couldn't move to defend himself as the barrel pointed to his head.

Then Ture jerked it and shot behind him.

He turned to see Bristol sinking to the floor as a blaster fell from his hands.

Ture collapsed against him. "He was going to shoot you in the back with the blaster Hauk handed him to defend himself with."

Slack-jawed, Hauk looked at Darling then Maris and finally Ture. "You said brother."

Ture swallowed hard. "He was."

Maris's heart shattered at those words. For him, Ture had killed his own brother. Before he could stop himself, he opened the face shield on his helmet and kissed him.

"Guys!" Hauk shouted. "We need to get out of here while we can. Put it back in your pants. Let's go!"

"I still have three charges," Darling told Hauk. "It should get us to the bay."

Maris pulled away and made sure to keep Ture by his side as they headed toward their shuttle. Like a mother hen, Darling guarded them while Hauk went first as their scout.

They were halfway there when Caillen's voice came over the link.

"We have company, and they're throwing us a welcome party."

Maris flinched at the sound of blaster fire and Fain's curses. He closed his face shield then shrugged his blast resistant jacket off and put it on Ture. It wasn't as much protection as he'd like, but it was better than nothing. He inclined his head to Hauk to cover them as they moved forward with Darling covering their backs.

When they reached the bay, it was crawling with League personnel. His heart hammering, Maris knew he couldn't carry Ture with his current wounds, and Ture was in no condition to run. "Hauk? Darling? Take Ture and get him on board. I'll draw fire."

Darling cursed at him.

"You sure?" Hauk asked.

"Yeah."

Ture went pale. "Mari?"

He cupped Ture's cheek as a wave of regret washed through him. *I want to make it back to you. . .*

But there was a lot of fire power here.

"Go with them, baby. I'll be right behind you."

He saw the doubt in Ture's gray eyes as Hauk took his own jacket off. Tossing Ture over his shoulder, Hauk used his jacket to shield Ture's legs. "On three I'm running to the shuttle with Ture," Hauk announced to the Sentella members who were with them. "Don't shoot us and someone open the damn door."

"On it," Caillen said.

Darling pulled out his bombs. "I'll deflect them with two charges."

Maris took one last look at Ture's damaged face and prayed for a miracle. When Hauk hit two, Maris jerked his helmet off so that the League would know he was the primary target they were after. He set it on Ture's head to protect him then ran into the bay before the others could stop him from doing it.

Darling's profanity echoed in his ears as Darling tried to cover him.

"Sulle!" one of their enemies shouted before they opened fire.

Darling's two charges went off, forcing them back temporarily.

Maris ran between ships and docked cargo, away from the shuttle, making sure that the soldiers had a clean line of sight on him.

"Damn it, Mari!" Darling shouted through the link in his ear. "Where did you vanish to? And what the fuck are you doing?"

"Protecting what I love. Don't worry about me, Darling. I want you to launch as soon as Ture's on board."

Darling went into a round of Phrixian curses that would have made Maris's father proud.

"Hauks, get Darling on that ship even if you have to shoot him. Fain, sit on his ass tight." Maris ducked as a plasma blast whizzed by his head. "Lock it down and get out."

Maris ran toward a large stack of boxes. Hitting his knees, he skidded around and opened fire on the soldiers who were closing in on his back. Then he jumped up and dove for cover.

And slammed against a League assassin.

Shit. . .

He waited for death. Until the assassin opened his helm.

It was Safir, who'd led them here to save Ture.

Maris scowled at his brother. Saf was supposed to have left already. "What are you doing?"

Saf handed him his blaster. "Use me as your shield."

"Are you insane?"

"No. I'm repaying a blood debt. At least partially. Now, do it, Maris, or I'll have to kill you."

Still, he hesitated. "If I do this, you'll lose your rank."

"Better than losing my brother." Saf closed his shield. "Don't worry about me, Mari. I'll live. Just get the others out. You know your crew will never leave you here to die and the League will never let any of you live."

Saf was right.

His heart breaking over what he had to do, Maris pulled him into a hug before he stepped around to Saf's back and grabbed his neck. "Darling? Are you in?"

"On the ramp, looking for your stupid ass. We're not leaving you, Mari. Ever."

He'd been a fool to think they would. But then, that was why they were family.

Family hung together, even when it was insane to do so. They didn't leave each other to die.

"I'm on my way."

Saf pretended to struggle as Maris dragged him toward the ship. While assassins were trained to kill each other in a situation like this, the men in the bay were foot soldiers. They wouldn't shoot so long as Maris held one of their own.

"I love you, brother," he whispered to Saf.

Saf squeezed his arm to let him know he felt the same way.

Maris hesitated as he reached the ramp. Kyr would have Saf beaten and stripped of his rank for this. They both knew it. But if Saf allowed Maris to escape without injury done to him, his punishment would be death.

Pressing his cheek against Saf's helmet, Maris held his brother close. He wanted to take Saf with him, but that would be even worse. Then Saf would be marked for death and hunted by every assassin the League had. It'd be kinder to shoot him in the head himself than relegate his brother to that fate.

"Shoot him!" Saf yelled to the other soldiers, covering his ass.

When one of the soldiers came close enough, Darling set off his last charge.

As it erupted, Maris pushed Saf away from it and down the ramp. With a deep breath for courage, he shot Saf in the shoulder then ran the rest of the distance up the ramp.

Darling and Hauk met him at the top. Hauk slammed and held him against the steel wall as Caillen launched their ship before the ramp finished closing.

Darling held on to a strap on the opposite side.

Hauk tightened his grip on Maris. "Ture's strapped in beside Caillen."

Maris patted his arm. "Thank you, Hauk. For everything."

"Any time, buddy."

Darling held his hand out for Maris to take. They didn't say a word to each other.

They didn't have to.

Through thick and thin, brothers to the bitter end.

The ship turned sharply as Caillen outmaneuvered their pursuers. How Hauk managed to keep him pinned to the wall, Maris had no idea. Damn, the Andarion was strong.

As they reached escape velocity, Nykyrian, Syn, Nero, Jayne and Fain brought their fighters in to engage the smaller ships after them.

Hauk released him. Maris made his way to the bridge where Chayden provided cover fire while Caillen piloted the ship. He barely saw them as his gaze locked on Ture. Rushing to him, he sank to his knees, threw his arms around Ture's waist and laid his head in his lap.

Ture brushed his hand through Maris's damp hair as tears blinded him. "You ever risk your life like that again, and I'll make Darling beat you."

"Copy that," Darling growled. "Only I'm allowed to be that stupid."

Maris laughed at them. He lifted his head to see Darling going over their settings. "What happened to Saf?"

"He's en route to the hospital and is suspended, pending investigation."

"Don't worry, Mari," Nykyrian said over the line. "Kyr will have him punished, but he won't kill him."

"Are you sure?"

"Positive. He won't trust Safir in the foreseeable future. However, he will know that one of two things happened.

Either you got the drop on your brother and used him, and you're not worth the loss of a highly trained assassin who has family loyalty to him. Or Saf helped you, and you now owe a blood debt to him. *That*, Kyr can use to trap you in the future."

And that was why Nykyrian was still alive, even though the League wanted him dead. It was frightening how much he understood the intricacies of other species and their politics.

Darling glanced over to him and offered a smile. "We also have one of our spies covering Saf's back. If anyone makes a move on him, we will get him out immediately. I promise you, no one's going to hurt your brother."

"Thank you." Maris looked up at Ture. "Are you all right?"

"Now that you're safe, I am."

Maris treasured those words as he forced his thoughts away from the tragedy of the night. The League had dealt them a hard blow.

Ture's brother was dead.

Because of me.

Taking Ture's hand, he held it to his lips as that harsh reality sank in. No one, other than Darling or Saf, would have protected him like that. It was something he'd never forget.

"I love you," he breathed.

A single tear fell down Ture's cheek. "Love you, too."

For the first time in his life, Maris knew it wasn't lip service.

This was real.

And it would be forever.

"Darling?"

"Yeah?"

Maris laughed as both Darling and Ture answered him. True to his promise, Ture never took offense to the times Maris called him 'darling.' Rather, he took it as the endearment it was meant to be, and never assumed Maris was calling him by the wrong name.

"Ture," he said with a smile to clarify who he was talking to. "The emperor has offered to allow us to live in the palace with his guard. Will you move in with me?"

Ture smiled. "Of course, I will. Have you seen the idiotic chances you take? I never intend to leave you alone again. I can't afford to."

Maris laughed. "Good. Otherwise, I was afraid you were about to relegate me to crazy stalker status."

Tightening his hand on Maris's, Ture shook his head. Until another thought hit him. "Where's Terek?"

"Jayne's husband has him. He wasn't hurt, and he was fed and sleeping when I checked in."

Ture let out a relieved breath. "You know, you're still listed as his legal father, and Ana had no other family. I have the custodial termination papers she had drawn up, but. . ."

Maris's breath caught in his throat as he hoped Ture was asking what he thought he was. "You want to keep him?"

"I would love to. You?"

Maris nodded. "I've always wanted to be a mom to someone other than Darling and his wayward siblings."

They all laughed at that.

Maris locked gazes with Ture. "You know, this officially makes us a family, right?"

Ture glanced over to Darling then to Hauk. "I think we were a family long before this."

"Just don't make me the creepy uncle," Hauk said. "Remember, we have Fain for that."

Snorting, Maris swept his gaze over some of the handful of people who meant everything to him. No, they weren't related by blood. But they were bound by something a lot stronger, and more powerful.

Mutual love and respect. And that was the only thing in the universe that was truly indestructible.

He'd spent the whole of his life trying to find someplace he belonged. Now he had it, and it was so much better than any of his dreams.

No, the people around him weren't perfect. Neither was he. But they tried and they loved him.

Just as he loved them.

That was all that really mattered. It was the best anyone could hope for and right now, he knew one undeniable truth. . ..

He really was the luckiest bitch in the universe.

And as long as he had Ture and their son with him, nothing else would ever matter more.

About Sherrilyn Kenyon

The #1 *New York Times* bestselling author, Sherrilyn Kenyon, who is proud of her mixed Cherokee heritage, lives a life of extraordinary danger. . . as does any woman with three sons, a husband, a menagerie of pets and a collection of swords that all of the above have a major fixation with. But when not running interference (or dashing off to the emergency room), she's found chained to her computer where she likes to play with all her imaginary friends. With more than thirty million copies of her books in print, in over one hundred countries, she certainly has a lot of friends to play with too.

In the past three years, her books have claimed the coveted #1 bestselling spot sixteen times. This extraordinary bestseller continues to top every genre she writes. Her current series include: The Dark-Hunters, The League, and Chronicles of Nick. Since 2004, she has placed more than 60 novels on the *New York Times* list in all formats including manga.

Her Lords of Avalon novels have been adapted by Marvel and her Dark-Hunter novels are now a New York Times bestselling manga published by St. Martins. Her Chronicles of Nick and Dark-Hunter series are both soon to be a major motion picture releases. For more information, visit her online at sherrilynkenyon.com.

Don't miss the next exciting League adventure. . .

Born of Fury

Coming 2014

The war is on. . .

Counted among the fiercest Andarion warriors ever born, Hauk is one of the five founding members of the Sentella—an organization that has declared war on the League that rules the Ichidian universe with an iron fist and terrifies it with an army of well-trained assassins. Hauk's enemies are legion, but he fears nothing and no one. He will do whatever it takes to survive and protect his Sentella brethren.

Sumi Antaxas is one of the best assassins the League has ever trained. In her world, failure is not an option and she has never met a target she couldn't execute. So when she's assigned Hauk, she believes it'll be a quick and easy mission.

But nothing is ever as simple as it seems, and Hauk is far better trained and skilled than his dossier shows. More than that, as she pursues him, she stumbles upon the key that will bring down not only Hauk, but the entire Sentella organization—and end the lives of its High Command.

In the race to report her information, Sumi is overtaken by enemies out to kill her as effectively as she intends to kill Hauk. Now her only key to survival is the one man she's been sent to terminate. And Hauk doesn't trust her at all.

The only question is—will he help her to live. . . or send her to her grave.

From the world of Dark-Hunter. . .

STYXX

Coming 9/3/2013

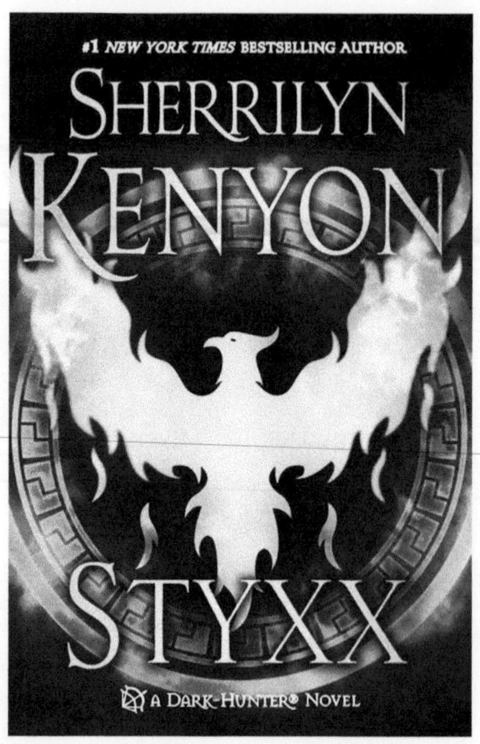

JUST WHEN YOU THOUGHT DOOMSDAY WAS OVER. . .

CENTURIES AGO ACHERON SAVED THE human race by imprisoning an ancient evil bent on absolute destruction. Now that evil has been unleashed and it is out for revenge.

As the twin to Acheron, Styxx hasn't always been on his brother's side. They've spent more centuries going at each other's throats than protecting their backs. Now Styxx has a chance to prove his loyalty to his brother, but only if he's willing to trade his life and future for Acheron's.

The Atlantean goddess of Wrath and Misery, Bethany was born to right wrongs. But it was never a task she relished.

Until now.

She owes Acheron a debt that she vows to repay, no matter what it takes. He will join their fellow gods in hell and nothing is going to stop her.

But things are never what they seem, and Acheron is no longer the last of his line. Styxx and Acheron must put aside their past and learn to trust each other or more will suffer.

Yet it's hard to risk your own life for someone who once tried to take yours, even when it's your own twin, and when loyalties are skewed and no one can be trusted, not even yourself, how do you find a way back from the darkness that wants to consume the entire world?

One that wants to start by devouring your very soul?

CONTINUE TO THE NEXT PAGE FOR AN EXCLUSIVE SNEAK PEEK...

June 23, 9548 BC

King Xerxes stared down at the infant boy who peacefully slept in his arms. How could his joy have turned so bitter so fast? For a moment, he'd believed himself to be the most blessed of all kings. That the gods had granted him two sons to rule his vast empire.

Now. . .

Did he even have one?

There was no doubt that the firstborn, Acheron, was born of the gods. That his wife-queen had whored herself to them and birthed it.

But Styxx. . .

The king studied every inch of the perfect, sleeping child nestled against his body. "Are you mine?" He was desperate to know the truth.

The infant appeared to be a mere human babe. Unlike Acheron, whose eyes swirled a living silver color, Styxx's were vivid blue and perfect. But then the gods were ever treacherous.

Ever deceitful.

Could it be that Acheron was his son and this one was not? Or that neither child belonged to him?

He looked to the elder wise woman who'd proclaimed

Acheron a god's son just after his birth. Decrepit and wizened, she wore heavy white robes that were richly embroidered in gold. Her gray hair was wrapped around an ornate gold crown. "Who is the father of this child?"

The woman paused in her cleaning. "Majesty, why do you ask me something you already know?"

Because he didn't know. Not for certain. And he hated the taste of fear that scalded his throat and left it bitter. Fear that made his heart pound in trepidation. "Answer me, woman!"

"Truth or lie, will you believe whatever answer I give?"

Damn her for her sagacity. How could the gods have done this to him? He'd sacrificed and prayed to them his whole life. Devoutly and without blasphemy. Why would they taint his heir in this manner?

Or worse, take his heir from him?

He tightened his grip, which caused the baby to wake and cry out. A part of him wanted to slam the child into the ground and watch it die. To stomp it into oblivion.

But what if this one *was* his son? His own flesh and blood. . .

The wise woman had said it was.

However, she merely relayed what the gods told her, and what if *they* lied?

Angry and betrayed, he went to the woman and shoved the infant into her arms. Let someone else solace it for now. He couldn't bear the sight of either child.

Without another word, he stormed from the room.

The moment she was alone with the babe, the old crone transformed into a beautiful young woman with long black hair. Dressed in bloodred, she placed a kiss to the boy's head and he instantly calmed down.

"Poor, poor Styxx," the goddess Athena whispered as she rocked him in her arms to soothe him. "Like your brother, yours will be an unpleasant future. I'm sorry I couldn't do more for either of you. But the human world needs her heroes. And one day, they will all need you."

March 10, 9543 BC

Five years later

"YOU WRETCHED LITTLE THIEF!"

Styxx looked up at the shrill cry of his older sister. Ryssa towered above him and his twin brother Acheron as they played with their wooden horses and soldiers on the floor.

Why was she always so cross at him? No matter what he did to try and please her, it was never enough.

Ryssa hated him. She always had.

"I took nothing."

Curling her lip, she closed the distance between them and yanked him up from the floor by his arm. "Where did you put it, you worthless little worm?" she demanded, shaking him so hard it felt as if she'd rip his arm off.

Styxx tried to break free, but she was too strong for him. "Put what?"

"The toy horse Father gave me for my birthday. I know you collect them and I know you stole mine. Where is it?"

"I haven't touched it."

"You're such a liar!" She threw him toward the ground

then went to search his things again. “Where have you hidden it?”

Styxx met Acheron’s gaze. “Did you take it?” he whispered to his brother.

Acheron shook his head.

Then who?

“What are you doing in here?”

All of them froze at the sound of fury in their nurse’s voice. Before Styxx could explain that he’d invited Acheron in to play with him, the nurse snatched his brother away.

Acheron cried out as the nurse’s grip bit into his small arm. “How many times have you been told to stay in your own room?”

Styxx panicked as he realized Acheron still held one of the soldiers in his hand. Even though he’d given them to his brother, he knew what would happen if anyone saw it in Acheron’s possession.

His brother would be punished. Again.

Wanting only to protect Acheron, Styxx launched himself from the floor and grabbed it out of Acheron’s hand.

Acheron offered him a small smile of gratitude before he was taken away.

“You!” Ryssa sneered as she glared at the toy he held. “You’re so selfish. You never think of anyone but yourself. What would it have hurt to let him keep one toy? Huh?” She gestured to the others scattered on the ground. “Nothing’s ever enough for you, is it? You always want more and you don’t care who you take it from.”

She jerked the toy from his hand, cutting his palm in the process, and stormed from his room.

Heartbroken, Styxx stood alone. He hated being by himself with a passion that made no sense. Ofttimes, he wondered if it came from being born a twin. Surely the gods wouldn’t have given him a brother if they meant for him to be forever by himself.

And yet, he spent very much of his life alone.

Sighing wistfully, Styxx glanced around the room

that was littered with toys. He would gladly give them all away if he could only have one person to play with. Ryssa refused because she didn't like him and he was a smelly boy, and, according to her, he was too stupid to follow the games she played with Acheron. The other children ran away from him because their parents were afraid they might hurt him, either by accident or on purpose, and incur his father's wrath.

Acheron was the only one who welcomed him as a playmate. But their father demanded they stay separated.

Styxx looked down at his brother's toy and wished with everything he had that it was different for them both. Rather they'd been born poor farmers than have to endure the burden of this wretched family and its meanness.

He set the toy aside. Later, after everyone was asleep, he'd return it to his brother.

“Acheron?” Styxx whispered, nudging his sleeping brother awake.

Slowly, Acheron blinked his eyes open. Rubbing them with his fist, Acheron sat up in bed. Styxx shoved the loaf of sweet bread in his face, making Acheron smile the moment he saw it.

“I didn't bring the honey, sorry. But. . .” Styxx opened his small cloth bag to show the sugared figs he'd taken. “I managed to pilfer your favorite.”

Acheron's silver eyes lit up. “Thank you! But you shouldn't have. You could have been caught.”

Styxx shrugged. “I wouldn't have been hurt over this.” At least not physically—those beatings were reserved for other offenses. Though there were times when he'd prefer being hit to listening to them call him worthless or other names.

Glad he'd helped his brother, Styxx watched as Acheron tore into the bread. Since they'd sent them both to bed with no supper, Acheron was starving. But as usual, Styxx had been unable to sleep and so once the palace quieted down, he'd snuck to the pantry.

"What did you eat?" Acheron asked.

"Bread. . .with your honey." He grinned wide with his guilt.

Acheron laughed. "That was wrong of you."

Styxx indicated the small bag. "I thought you'd rather have the figs."

"You could have given me the choice."

"And I would have, had my belly not been cramping. It smelled so good, I couldn't take it anymore. I had to eat some on my way here. Sorry."

"Then I shall forgive you." Acheron held the bread out. "Would you like more?"

He shook his head, declining it. Even though he was still hungry, he knew Acheron was even more so.

Frowning while he ate, Acheron cocked his head. "Can you not sleep again?"

"I tried." Morpheus held a grudge against him for reasons only the gods knew. No matter how hard Styxx tried, sleep forever eluded him.

Acheron scooted back on his pallet, making more room.

Grateful beyond measure, Styxx accepted his unspoken invitation and lay down by Acheron's side.

Within a few minutes, he was sound asleep. Acheron finished his food then tucked the bag into Styxx's chiton. Licking the last of the sugar from his fingers, he curled up behind Styxx, back to back, and placed the bottoms of his feet flush to his brother's. As far back as he could remember they had slept like this whenever they could. Neither of them liked to be alone or apart, and yet their family seemed determined for them to be so. It was something neither of them understood.

How they both wished they could be left alone together.

And Styxx was the one he loved best.

His brother was the only one who treated him like he was normal. Styxx didn't hate him like their parents did, nor dote on him like he was a god incarnate as Ryssa was prone to do.

They were brothers. They played. They laughed. And they fought for everything they were worth. But whenever the fighting was done, they would dust off and be friends again.

Always and forever.

Closing his eyes, Acheron heard the voices that were always in his head. Styxx heard them, too. But while Acheron only heard those of the gods, Styxx heard those and many, many more. It was one of the reasons his brother had such difficulty sleeping. Whenever they were together, the voices in Styxx's head stopped shouting at him and left him free to rest. Styxx could only hear Acheron's thoughts then, and Acheron was very careful of them.

But the moment they were apart, the voices returned to Styxx with a vengeance. The constant lack of sleep made his twin irritable most days and gave him terrible headaches. Headaches so ferocious that at times his nose bled from them, and he was often sick to his stomach.

No one else understood that. They accused Styxx of faking the pain. And both of them were terrified of telling others what they heard. Everyone but Styxx hated him enough already. Acheron had no desire to give them another cause.

When Styxx had tried to tell others about the voices, he'd been ridiculed and punished for lying. Even Ryssa had accused him of making it up for attention. So both of them had learned to keep the secret and tell no one. Ever.

There were many secrets the two of them shared.

And they had promised each other that one day, when they were grown and no one could stop them, they would leave this place and go somewhere else where people didn't treat them so badly.

Like his twin brother, Acheron couldn't wait for that day to come.

May 9, 9542 BC

"Sit up straight! You slouch like a fishmonger's son."

Styxx flinched at his father's angry tone and straightened himself immediately in his uncomfortable gold chair where his legs had gone numb from dangling over the edge of it. But if he folded them under him, it would anger his father even more than his slouching. While his father often doted on him, especially whenever they were in public, there were other times when his father would be so cross that nothing he did pleased him. Times when his father seemed to begrudge him every breath he took.

Today was definitely one of those days.

"Are we boring you, boy?"

Styxx shook his head quickly, resisting the urge to groan out loud as pain split his skull with absolute agony. He'd always hated his headaches and the one today was more excruciating than normal. It made it impossible to focus. Worse, he felt as if he would vomit at any moment. *That* his father would find unforgivable.

What? Are you a pregnant woman, boy? You vomit as such. Learn to control your stomach. You're to be a man, for the gods' sakes. Men don't throw up every other minute. They control themselves and their bodies at all times.

His stomach heaved violently, sending more pain throbbing through his head, which then sickened him all the more. The constant seesawing between his head and stomach was enough to make him want to scream in agony.

"Might I be excused, Father?"

His father turned to glare at him furiously. "To what purpose?"

"I don't feel well." That was a substantial understatement.

"Come here."

Styxx scooted off his small throne and resisted the urge to wince as a thousand needles stabbed at his sleeping legs. Knowing better than to let his father see the pain it caused him, he crossed the dais to his father's huge gilded throne. It was so massive that the top of his blond head barely reached the arm of it. Dressed in a white and purple stola and chlamys that matched Styxx's chiton; his father's blond hair and beard gleamed in the light beneath the gold-leaf crown that would one day be Styxx's.

As they always did on this day of every week, they'd spent all morning dealing with the problems and concerns of the nobles and people who wanted an audience with their king. Since this was something Styxx would have to do once he ruled this kingdom, for the last year his father had made him stay and listen so that he could use his father's wisdom once he inherited the crown. While Styxx was here, he was never to move or speak. Only observe.

The "privilege" of attending these sessions had been his sole birthday gift last summer when he'd turned five.

With a fierce frown creasing his forehead, his father touched Styxx's brow. "You have no fever. What are your symptoms?"

"My head aches."

He rolled his eyes. "And?"

I want to vomit and I'm terribly dizzy. But he knew from experience that his father would only ridicule those complaints.

"That is all, Father. But the pain is ferocious."

His father glared at him. "You will one day be king, boy. Do you think they will stop a war or an uprising because you have a meager headache?"

"No, Sire."

"That is correct. The world does not stop for something so trivial. Now sit and listen. Observe your future duties. Your people are far more important than your boredom and they deserve your full attention."

But it wasn't boredom. Every shred of light or hint of sound pierced his head with a pain so foul that he wanted to bash his own brains in. Why could no one ever understand his headaches and how much they hurt?

Tears of pain and frustration formed, but he quickly blinked them away. He'd learned long ago that while his father would console Ryssa whenever she cried, he would never tolerate tears from his son. Styxx was to be a man, not some mollycoddled girl. . .

Trying not to jar his head while he moved, Styxx returned to his seat.

"Sit up!" his father barked instantly.

Styxx jerked upright then winced in pain. *Don't show it. . .*

But it was so hard not to. Swallowing in agony, he glanced out the window to see Ryssa in the garden with Acheron. They were laughing as they chased each other and played. What he wouldn't give to be outside with them in the beautiful sunshine.

Not that it would matter. Even if his head didn't hurt, Ryssa would never swing him around like that. She'd never laugh with him or tickle him. Her love was reserved solely for Acheron.

Turning his head, he tried not to think about it as another wave of misery pierced his brain.

Styxx leaned forward at the same time blood poured from his nose. N*o! Please, not now. . .Please, gods.* He pressed his hand to his nose, trying to stanch it before his father took note.

“Majesty? Is His Highness all right?”

Styxx panicked at the guard’s question that brought his father’s full attention back to him.

Rage darkened his father’s brow. “Did you do that on purpose?”

Yes, I purposefully cut open my nose with no means whatsoever just to spite you, Father. I’m truly talented that way.

“No, Father. I shall be all right. It’s just another nosebleed. It will stop in a few minutes.”

The king curled his lip in disgust. “Look at you! You’re filthy. You don’t dishonor those around you or your divinely given station with such sanguinariness.” The king jerked his chin at the guard who’d ratted him out and Styxx’s valet who was charged with keeping him immaculate and presentable any time he was in public. “Take the prince to his room and see that he’s cleaned and changed.”

Great, I sound like an infant or puppy.

They bowed low before crossing the room to stand before Styxx.

Already dreading what this would mean for him later, Styxx kept his nostrils pinched together and slid off his seat, then headed for his room upstairs. As he crossed the atrium from the throne room toward the main palace, he paused again to watch Acheron and Ryssa laughing and playing in the back garden. The bleeding in his nose worsened as did the voices that shouted even louder than before.

Tears filled his eyes. He wanted to scream from it all, and when Acheron fell and scraped their knees, Styxx couldn’t take it anymore. He hit the ground, clutching his leg and crying out as his pain finally overwhelmed him completely.

Please, gods, please just let me die. . .

Acheron came running to his side. “Styxx? Are you all right?”

No. I live in a state of constant physical pain no one understands or has mercy for. And he was tired of it. Dear gods, could he not have one single hour where something didn't hurt?

"Styxx?"

He couldn't respond to his brother, not while he ached so badly and in so many ways. Instead, he stared at the blood on Acheron's ravaged skin. He felt the same exact injury on his own knee and yet he knew that if he looked at his leg, he'd have no wound to explain the throbbing ache he felt there.

"Don't get hurt again, Acheron," Styxx finally breathed. "Please."

Acheron frowned as Ryssa came forward. She knelt on the ground by Styxx's side. "Why are you lying here?"

Styxx pushed himself up before she could mock his pain, too. "I fell."

She glanced around the path. "There's nothing for you to trip over. What? You saw Acheron fall and couldn't stand him getting five seconds more of attention than you?"

Styxx glared at her as more agony split his skull. "Yes, that's exactly what happened."

"Have you another headache?" Acheron asked.

Styxx nodded then winced.

Ryssa scoffed. "Father says you only pretend to have them to get out of your responsibilities."

He gestured toward his soiled chiton. "What of the blood that covers me?"

"You probably injured yourself for sympathy. I know you. You're not above doing anything for attention."

That was so him. . .never.

Unable to deal with her criticism, Styxx cradled his aching skull in the palm of his right hand and continued on to his room with his valet and guard trailing in his wake.

Acheron started to follow after him, but Ryssa held him back.

"Let him go, Acheron. He'll just get you into trouble like he always does. Come. Let us play more."

Hours later, Styxx lay in bed, trying his best not to move or breathe. Suddenly, he felt a gentle hand in his hair. He knew instantly who it was. Only one person was that kind or caring where he was concerned.

"Acheron?" he whispered.

Without answering, his brother crawled into bed behind him. "Is your head any better?"

"Not really. Yours?"

"It hurts but not as much as yours, I think. I can still function with mine." Acheron touched the fresh bruises on Styxx's bare back that throbbed even more than his head did. "Why were you punished?"

"I left the court sessions early. Like Ryssa, Father didn't believe my head hurts. He thought I was trying to avoid my responsibilities." Something their father had absolutely no tolerance for.

Acheron put his arms around him and held him close. "I'm sorry, Styxx."

"Thank you." Styxx didn't speak for several minutes as the voices in his head finally grew fainter and the cranial ache lessened enough that he could almost breathe normally again. "Acheron? Why do you think I can feel your pain, but you don't feel mine?"

"Ryssa would say it's the will of the gods."

But why? Styxx suspected that he must not be as important to the gods as Acheron. Why else would he feel his brother's wounds while Acheron was impervious to his pain? It was as if the gods wanted to ensure that Styxx protected his brother from all harm. As if he was Acheron's divinely chosen whipping boy. . .

"What do you believe, Acheron?"

"I don't know. Any more than I understand why the gods have abandoned us to such awful people while they speak so loudly in our heads. It doesn't make sense, does it?" Acheron turned over and pressed his back to Styxx's, then his feet. As they lay quietly in the darkness of Styxx's room, Acheron reached to take Styxx's hand into his. "I'm sorry Ryssa is so mean to you. She just thinks that you're doted on and spoiled while they treat me badly."

"What do you think?"

"I see the truth. Our parents are suspicious of you, too. And while they are nice to you at times, they're also very, very mean."

Yes, they were. And unlike Acheron, he couldn't complain about it. No one believed him when he did so. They accused him of being spoiled and then disregarded his pain as insignificant, or worse, they took perverse pleasure in his suffering as if he deserved it because he was a prince while they were not. Sometimes he thought it would be better to be Acheron. At least his brother knew what reception he'd receive whenever their parents were around. Styxx never knew until it was too late.

Sometimes his father was loving, and then at others. . .

He lashed out as if he hated Styxx even more than he hated Acheron. It made no sense and was terribly confusing to his young mind. For that reason, he didn't want to be around either of his parents or his sister.

It was best to avoid them and the confusion they caused.

Sighing, he squeezed Acheron's hand and let that touch silence the voices that urged him to kill himself. They were merciless in their taunts.

You are poison. So long as you live, you will suffer!

But if he died, Acheron died, too. The wise woman had proclaimed it so when they were born. Their lives had been joined together by the gods themselves and there was no way to undo it.

Maybe that is why you suffer.

The gods were trying to make him kill Acheron. To hate his brother so that Styxx would murder them both. It made sense in a way. Maybe they thought that if they tortured Styxx enough, he'd grow so tired of it that he'd be desperate enough to kill Acheron to end his own agony. Was that why their eyes were different? So that if he killed his brother, he wouldn't be looking into his own blue eyes when he did it?

Yet he couldn't make himself hate the only person who loved him. The only person who could comfort him and quiet the evil in his head.

Gods or no gods, misery or happiness, Acheron was his brother. Forever and always. He was the only real family Styxx had.

And the one thing he'd learned in his short life was that he couldn't trust anyone. Not even the gods. People lied all around him. Constantly. Even about the little things. Only Acheron was trustworthy and honest. Only his brother didn't try to harm him or seek to betray him to his father. So how could he hurt the only person in his life who treated him as something more than an object to be despised? The one person who didn't smirk in silent satisfaction whenever he was harmed?

"I love you, Acheron."

"I love you, too, brother."

Styxx leaned his head back until it rested against Acheron's and finally let the tears fall that had been misting his eyes all day. He could show them to Acheron. His brother understood and would never mock him for them. "Do you think we'll ever be able to leave this place and find peace?"

"No. I think we were born to suffer."

The saddest part? So did he. "At least we have each other."

Acheron nodded. "Brothers—always and forever. They'll never be able to take that away from us."